WAVES OF VENGEANCE

Judith Blevins A NOVEL
and Carroll Multz

Judith Blevins

Carroll Multz

WAVES OF VENGEANCE

Published by
ShahrazaD Publishing
859 Quail Run Dr.
Grand Junction, CO 81505

ISBN – 978-163732328-1

Contact the authors at:
judyblevins@bresnan.net
carrollmultz@charter.net

ALSO BY THE AUTHORS

Novels

By Judith Blevins

Double Jeopardy • *Swan Song*
Legacy • *Karma* • *Paragon*

By Carroll Multz

Justice Denied • *Deadly Deception* • *License to Convict*
The Devil's Scribe • *The Chameleon*
Shades of Innocence • *The Winning Ticket*

By Judith Blevins & Carroll Multz

Rogue Justice • *The Plagiarist* • *A Desperate Plea*
Spiderweb • *The Méjico Connection*
Eyewitness • *Lust for Revenge* • *Kamanda*
Bloodline • *Pickpocket* • *Ghost Writer*
Guilt by Innuendo • *Gypsy Card Reader*

Childhood Legends Series®
By Judith Blevins & Carroll Multz

Operation Cat Tale • *One Frightful Day* • *Blue*
The Ghost of Bradbury Mansion • *White Out*
Flash of Red • *Back in Time* • *Treasure Seekers*
Summer Vacation-Part 1: Castaways-Part 2: Blast Off
A Trip to Remember —The R*U*1*2s Journey
to the Nation's Capital

Dedication

To Margie Vollmer Rabdau
whose memory will long
be an inspiration and
without whom our novels
will not be the same.

The spurned,
by being vindictive,
generate no sympathy
only verification
of their unworthiness.

TABLE OF CONTENTS

A Note From The Authors

At one time, the determination for us was what novels to read; now it's what novel to write next. There's always a backlog of plots lurking in the recesses of our minds. In deciding which one to write next, we try to have it coincide with current events and one that is of grave public interest and concern. Sometimes that concern is public safety and the quest for the speedy and effective administration of justice. Oftentimes, it's to expose the turmoil caused by violence and not sugar coat it nor in anyway condone it. A murder mystery would not be a murder mystery without murder.

Since violence has become a large part of everyday life in various forms, we decided to go down a different path in writing *Waves of Vengeance*. It is not intended to be a blueprint for what to do and what not to do in committing the perfect crime. We still aspire to the old adages that what you sow, so shall you reap, and no bad deed should go unpunished! In a civilized society, disputes should be settled peacefully and not by a duel at sunrise.

Being in the midst of the Coronavirus lockdown, we have suspended our book signings but not our writing. This will be our fourth novel published during the pandemic with another on the way. Hopefully, sitting in your favorite recliner reading this and our other novels will make the restrictions more bearable. Stay safe and vigilant. Happy reading!

As we've often said, publishing a novel is truly a team effort. Special thanks to Lisa Knudsen for her editing skills; Frank Addington, for the cover and interior book designs; and Emily Fleming and John Lukon of KC Book Manufacturing for printing *Waves of Vengeance*. And last but not least, to our readers, you continue to be our inspiration.

Prologue

Captain Mitchell McElroy and I met while we were stationed at the Naval Air Station North Island located on the Coronado Peninsula between San Diego Bay and the Pacific Ocean. Mitch, a Navy pilot, is a few months from completing a twenty-year hitch and looking forward to retiring. I'm nearing the end of my second four-year commitment.

Mitch is assigned to a Nimitz-class nuclear powered aircraft carrier, the USS *Theodore Roosevelt*. The name plate on my desk identifies me as *PO3 Samantha Lombardi*. My secretarial skills and assertive attitude earned me the position of administrative aide to the base commander. I don't mind being a desk jockey. It's an eight to five job with weekends off. The kind of military job most would envy.

Mitch and I dated off and on for three years, and when we finally decided to tie the knot, we were married in the chapel on base. Our comrades honored us with the traditional saber arch salute as we left the church. Our reception was highlighted by several champagne toasts and cutting of the wedding cake—which incidentally was a particularly good replica of the USS *Theodore Roosevelt*. I remember thinking as we cut into the flight deck that the cake must've been a real challenge for the bakers. A small contingent from the Navy band played romantic music and we danced well into *o-dark-thirty*. Among my most precious possessions are the videos and photographs of our wedding and reception. I have them stored in my sea trunk at the foot of our bed.

• • •

The *Roosevelt* is the fourth Nimitz-class aircraft carrier to be operated by nuclear power and is capable of running 20 or more years without refueling. That concept still boggles my mind. One afternoon, as Mitch and I are lunching on the patio at the *HooYah*, a popular seafood shack located close to the base, I ask him, "How can that be?"

Mitch pauses suspending a deep-fried shrimp in midair as he looks toward the pier where the carrier is docked. Mitch is Navy to the bone, and as he studies the carrier, the admiration in his eyes is undeniable. Finally popping the shrimp into his mouth, and in between chews, points to the ship and explains to me how nuclear power works on carriers. It's evident by the authoritative tone of his voice that he loves showing off his knowledge.

"The ships have onboard nuclear reactors. The reactor splits the atoms which release energy as heat. The heat creates steam, and the steam turns the propulsion turbines that power the propeller."

His explanation makes it sound simple enough if you're a nuclear engineer. However, the whole thing is still way above my comprehension.

Mitch continues to educate me. "Our fleet is not welcomed in many ports worldwide because of the environmental concerns over nuclear energy. It's not uncommon to be met by protesters who try to board our ships bent on interrupting our voyages and God knows what else."

. . .

Our base, the Naval Amphibious Base, is located in Coronado, California, one of the most beautiful areas in the continental United States. As you cross the bridge that separates Coronado from San Diego, you enter an entirely different environment leaving the hectic hubbub of city life behind. The small town of Coronado is independent of San Diego and reminds me of an exquisite tropical island where even the exotic gardenia grows wild. Although I'm not a California girl, I dearly love Coronado despite the occasional scary tremors. Coronado does, however, have one thing in common with the rest of California, it's a very expensive place to live so I live on base.

. . .

Coronado is best known for training Navy SEALs (SEAL is the acronym for Sea, Air and Land) and BUD/S (the acronym for Basic Underwater Demolition) at the amphibious base located here. The SEALs have been training at Coronado since 1945. The rigorous 24 weeks of hell originates at the Naval Special Warfare Center in Coronado. It consists of three weeks of orientation; seven weeks of physical conditioning; seven weeks of combat diving, and seven weeks of land warfare. If trainees can endure and complete a 500-yard swim in nine minutes; 100 pushups in two minutes; 100 sit-ups in two minutes; 20 pull-ups; and a 1.5 mile run in nine minutes they can proudly claim the title of U.S. Navy SEAL.

Although SEAL training is a major interest to most of the public who visit Coronado, the history of the Navy base at Coronado is in and of itself a fascinating narrative. It was commissioned in 1917, and in 1963, was officially recognized by a resolution of the House Armed Services Committee as the Birthplace of Naval Aviation.

The first Navy aircraft carrier, USS *Langley*, was constructed in 1924 and based at the Naval Aviation Station in San Diego. By 1935, North Island, located at the north end of the Coronado peninsula on San Diego Bay, became home base to the Pacific Fleet where three other carriers joined the USS *Langley*. They were the USS *Lexington*, USS *Saratoga* and USS *Ranger*.

During World War II, forces stationed at North Island included the Marines, Coast Guard, Army, Navy and Seabees. The United Service Organization, better known as the USO, hosted entertainment shows and bond drives weekly at the military bases featuring such stars as Bob Hope and the Marx Brothers. Bob Hope was frequently accompanied by famous glamorous movie stars. Seeing such icons as Marilyn Monroe in person obviously was quite a treat for the troops and quite a morale booster.

In 1948, Fighter Squadron 52 was based at North Island and designated as the Navy's first jet training squadron. Interesting enough, among those trained at the island was Lt. C. Yamada, the infamous Japanese aviator who later became the head of Japan's Naval aviation forces during WWII. So much for unwittingly aiding the enemy!

Chapter One

The Keys

Mitch and I both love living by the ocean, and before we were married, we talked about getting a place in the Florida Keys where we could enjoy our retirement away from city life. During his twenty-year stint in the Navy, Mitch became acquainted with members of the other branches of the armed services. Mitch told me that when he was single and carefree, he partied with some of the members of the amphibious variety. He still keeps in touch with a couple of them, especially Scott Cooper and Chip Larson, who likewise have retired from the service.

While still active in the SEALs, Scott was given the title *Bullfrog*. Although it sounds like an insult, the title is actually an honor and bestowed upon the SEAL with the most time in service upon completing training. Scott and Chip, having qualified as Navy Special Warfare Operators, both proudly wore a Trident badge. They referred to the badge as a *Budweiser* because the Trident resembles the eagle on the Budweiser beer can.

Almost every morning as the frogmen do laps past my office, I hear them chanting: *HooYah,*

HooYah, HooYah, HEY! Today's gonna be another easy day! Knowing what I know about their training, I'm not so sure the word easy is really such an apt description.

Mitch often spoke of a married couple, Mattie and Ray Fleming. Ray was also one of the fighter pilots assigned to the *Roosevelt.* Before we were married, and even before we started dating, Mattie would invite Mitch to dinner on a regular basis. Mitch and the Flemings become close friends. Ray retired from the service a few years before Mitch and he and Mattie bought a house in Key West.

• • •

The Florida Keys, situated between the Atlantic Ocean and the Gulf of Mexico, consists of a string of islands off the southern tip of Florida. The word key is from the Spanish word *cayo*, which means small island. Although Key Largo is the largest island in the grouping, Key West is thought to be the most desirable. When you consider there are over 800 islands in the coral cay archipelago, that's quite a compliment. For many years, Key West, being close to the Bahamas and Cuba, provided a trade route to New Orleans. Because of the strong currents and dangerous reefs, at one time shipwrecks along the route were a weekly occurrence. The subtropical climate in the Keys consists of balmy temperatures year-round, which even hover in the 70s in January.

The island of Key West is located in the Straits of Florida. Being the southernmost city in the U.S., it is connected to the mainland by the Overseas Highway. The Overseas Highway, stretching across a chain of coral and limestone islands, is one of the longest overwater highways in the world.

A small island measuring two miles by four miles, Key West is geographically located 159 miles south of Miami and 90 miles north of Cuba.

Although Key West is known for its luxury resorts, the island also boasts of historical museums, quaint curio shops, enticing restaurants and exotic bars that offer a variety of entertainment. Visitors to the island seem to be enchanted by the conch-style homes which are a unique blend of tropical and Victorian architecture. To add to their charm, most of the pastel-painted homes are graced by balconies. The median price of a modest home in the Keys is approximately a half million dollars.

The island is known for its coral reefs, diving and snorkeling. It is a popular stopover for cruise ships, has an international airport and a ferry that makes a daily run up the Atlantic coastline to Miami, Florida.

Needless to say, it's not all fun and games. During the summer months, or *mean season* as it's sometimes called, there's always the threat of hurricanes. And being a mere 90 miles from Cuba, Key West has a serious drug trafficking problem. It's been said that Key West is one of the most dangerous areas in the U.S. because it's an easy route into south Florida for drug smugglers.

• • •

Being on the cusp of closing out our Navy careers, we start looking for a place to settle permanently. We love Coronado but had previously ruled out making California our home upon retirement. Property is far too expensive in California, not to mention the fact that mini earthquakes occur almost daily and the threat of the *big one* is always on the horizon. We wanted to relocate close to the ocean and had previously considered living in Florida.

Apparently, retirement didn't work out too well for the Flemings and their marriage fell apart. Mitch had remained in touch with them throughout the years and when they learned he was retiring, they offered to sell him their Key West property at an affordable price.

Mitch is at loose ends having retired from the Navy two months before I complete my second four-year commitment. When we receive Ray's call, we decide to investigate his offer and Mitch drives to Key West to look at the Fleming property.

The day after Mitch arrives in Key West, he calls. "Honey, I love this place. Ray told me they have two other buyers standing in line willing to pay far more than the price he quoted us. But because of our friendship, he said he'd give us the opportunity to accept his offer. I couldn't refuse. I said yes, and guess what? We're now the proud owners of a lovely conch-style home in the Keys."

I'm stunned and disappointed that Mitch hadn't conferred with me before making such an important decision. When I remain silent, he says, "Ah, I know you're just gonna love it here."

. . .

Mitch returned to Coronado and as soon as I complete my commitment, we pack our belongings into a U-Haul and head for Key West. Two days later, we're standing barefoot on the beach in front of our new home admiring our purchase and the speculator view.

"It isn't much but at least it's ours," I say, trying to keep the disappointment out of my voice.

"Take heart, my dear," Mitch replies through a smile. "When we finish with the renovations, it's going to make the Taj look like a dive."

I slip my arm through Mitch's and snuggle close to him. I admire his upbeat attitude. He's usually right and I trust his judgment. However, comparing this fixer-upper to the Taj Mahal is quite a stretch.

• • •

Our *new* home was constructed in the 1920s. Mitch told me that Ray said before he, Ray, bought the house, he researched the history of the homes in the district that is known as Old Town. Curious as to why the homes held up so well during hurricanes, Ray told Mitch he discovered most were built of a hard wood known as Dade County pine, which is now virtually non-existent.

Ray also gave Mitch instructions on how to prepare for a hurricane. Mitch related their conversation as follows:

"I grew tired of covering the windows with plywood every time we received a hurricane warning, so I added shutters to all the windows. And surprisingly enough, they're effective," Ray told him.

"I noticed them," Mitch said he told Ray. "They're so attractive, I thought they were part of the decor."

"You'll learn to appreciate the convenience after your first hurricane warning," Mitch said Ray replied. "The way I designed them is that when shut they fit snugly inside the window frame. That lessens the chance of them being ripped from the house in high winds."

Mitch told me Ray went on to say, "When you do get hurricane warnings, make sure the loose items around the outside of the property are secure. Anything that can become a missile needs to be battened down, things such as trash cans and yard furniture. Also, coconuts can become deadly flying objects and should be harvested on a regular basis. If you don't want to climb the tree, you can use a pole pruner to remove them. It's awkward but it works.

"It's a good idea to have plenty of water, an updated generator, canned goods, snacks and flashlight batteries on hand at all times, and not just in anticipation of a hurricane. Keep some simple tools inside the house in case you need to do emergency repairs and can't access the garage."

Mitch told me his head was spinning after receiving the barrage of instructions. He said he jokingly asked Ray, "Is it too late to back out of the contract?"

Ray apparently laughed and replied, "Being prepared is ninety percent of the battle. Make it easy on yourself. Besides, we're not hit that often." Mitch said Ray then paused and added, "Remember, I had people standing in line to buy this place. If you're having byer's remorse, I'll gladly return your earnest money."

• • •

We spend the next three months making renovations both inside and out. We update the kitchen appliances, replace all the flooring with light-colored tile squares, paint the walls a soft eggshell and incorporate a tropical blend of rattan furniture accented with a mix of colorful floral cushions. Taking Ray's advice, we also designate space in the pantry for the provisions he suggested we have on hand in preparation for a hurricane or other disasters.

We opt to keep the same colors on the outside of the house as they blend in with the other pastels in the neighborhood. However, we give the pale pink exterior, white shutters and balcony railing a facelift by repainting them. Throughout the entire project, except for the electrical and plumbing updates, Mitch and I do the bulk of the work.

When we finally finish, we celebrate our new beginnings on the patio by dinning on grilled salmon and white wine. The tropical evening is calm and clear, and as we watch the surf ebb and flow, we can see several boats bobbing around on the ocean. We didn't know it at the time, but some of those boats were from Havana and their cargo consisted of illegal drugs.

"You were right," I say, and take Mitch's hand. "I do love it here."

Mitch affectionately squeezes my hand. "I knew you would." After a moment of silence, he says, "By the way, Sam, Casey dropped by this afternoon while you were shopping."

Casey operates a small airfield not far from Old Town where we live. My instincts tell me something's up, so I cautiously approach the inevitable. "So, Casey came by," I say more as a question than a comment.

"Yeah. So, Casey knows this old geezer who owns a vintage Piper Cub. Since the guy is the original owner, Casey can vouch for the plane's logged time and condition."

"Okay, bully for him," I say.

Mitch ignores my insolence, but I'm sure he got the message that I was getting the message.

"Well, the guy has fallen on hard times and needs to sell the plane. He's letting it go for a mere fifteen K," Mitch remarks and looks at me apparently hoping for a positive sign.

"Fifteen thousand dollars!" I blurt.

Mitch pounces, "Yeah, well considering used Pipers sell for between thirty and fifty thou, that's quite a steal."

"Un-huh. And pray tell me, where are we going

to get fifteen thousand dollars to buy a plane?" I ask.

"I figured that out already…"

"I just bet you have!" I smirk, still stinging as I remember him buying the Key West property without first consulting with me. I reason that since he was a flight captain and responsible for making split second decisions, that tendency carried over into his civilian life.

Again, ignoring my sarcasm, Mitch continues, "We didn't use all the money we had earmarked for the house renovation. By doing the work ourselves, we saved about ten grand. We can take the other five out of savings and pay ourselves back. Spread over a year that's about four hundred a month. We can do that, can't we?"

Listening to his plea, it suddenly hits me. *Mitch really has his heart set on this plane.* "Have you flown it?" I ask in a more conciliatory tone.

"Yes, last week when I went into town to pick up supplies, I ran by the airfield. Jason Weston, the geezer, was just landing the Piper. Casey must've mentioned to Jason that I might be interested in buying the plane. After Casey introduced us, Jason tossed me the keys and told me to take 'er up for a spin."

"Sounds like test driving a car," I say.

"Yep! Well, that's pilot talk for taking 'er up

for a spin." Mitch smiles apparently pleased at his humor. I just roll my eyes in mock disgust.

The moment passes and Mitch continues, "Sam, I really miss flying and I like being around aircraft, so I go by Casey's once in a while." The sadness in his voice is unmistakable.

Moved by his emotion, I say, "Guess we can put having a baby on hold."

WAVES OF VENGEANCE — JUDITH BLEVINS & CARROLL MULTZ

Chapter Two

Uno, Dos, Tres

At the age of twenty-one, Juan Santiago defected to the United States as part of a group of Cubans fleeing the dictatorial Castro regime. The day after his arrival, determined to embrace his new beginnings, Juan diligently sought employment in Miami. He soon learned that positions for unskilled labor were few. When a fellow refugee told him that work opportunities were far better in Key West, Juan wasted no time hitchhiking a ride south. A semi-truck driver, whose uniform name tag identified him as Carlos, picked him up. The truck was vintage but comfortable and Juan was grateful.

When Carlos asked Juan where he was going, Juan explained his circumstances.

"I make delivers from time-to-time to a wholesale fish distributor in Key West," Carlos said. "They may be looking for help. If you're interested…"

"I am, and thank you very much," Juan said in broken English.

When the pickup began the trek across the

Overseas Bridge between Miami and Key West, Juan, having never seen an overwater bridge, much less one of this magnitude, was mesmerized—and maybe a little terrified. *What if the bridge collapses?* he thought as he clung tightly to the handle above the door.

Much to Juan's relief, the truck made the crossing without incident. When Carlos stopped to refuel, he motioned for Juan to join him, and they went into the convenience store. Juan went to the restroom while Carlos bought them each a beef and bean burrito and a drink.

When Juan reappeared, Carlos said, "The clerk," then motioned to a teen standing behind the counter, "told me the fish distributer I mentioned is hiring. I'll drive you over there."

Juan couldn't believe his luck. "Muchas gracias," he replied through a mouthful of beef and bean burrito.

As it turned out, the fish distributer had several openings and hired Juan on the spot. Juan relished his job as it afforded him a decent salary and he felt, compared to his life in Cuba, that he was doing well. He was able to afford a small apartment just a couple of miles from work and he eventually picked up an old Ford beater.

• • •

Although not movie star handsome, Juan was nice looking. He was buff from lifting crates of fish on a daily basis. Most evenings found him trolling the hot spots in downtown Key West and not for fish. Carmen Ochoa was also a regular at the bars. Juan had noticed her on several occasions but was too shy to approach her. It was well known by the regulars that Carmen was not shy when it came to men, especially after a couple of drinks.

One evening as they sat at the bar, Carmen held up her empty glass, and gesturing in Juan's direction, asked, "Care to buy a lady a drink?"

She was attractive and did not try to hide her attributes. She used her good looks to manipulate men and soon she was dating Juan. The agreement between them was that Juan never pick her up at her home, her rules, not his. They always met elsewhere. Not having dated much in the past, it never occurred to Juan that this arrangement was unusual. He reasoned she probably didn't want her neighbors to know her business. He could relate to that.

Juan respected her privacy. After having had a bad experience as a teen, he was timid and apprehensive. As a high school student in Cuba, a fellow classmate lured Juan's one and only girlfriend, Lolita, away from him. Hurt, humiliated, and lacking self-confidence, Juan never dated again in high school, and because of being betrayed by one he thought was a friend and the other a girlfriend, he never discussed his personal life with anyone. Although he would like to have bragged about dating the desirable Carmen Ochoa, he didn't dare for fear someone would step in and she'd be whisked away.

Juan was instantly head-over-heels in love with Carmen and doted over her to an extreme. However, Carmen obviously was not smitten with Juan. Any outsider could tell she was just using him. He was so giddy over having a woman of her caliber in his life he was unable to think straight. Her wish was his command, and Juan depleted his savings lavishing Carmen with gifts in an attempt to curry her favor and keep her interested in their relationship.

• • •

Juan daydreamed of being married to Carmen. However, being shy and uneducated in matters of the heart, he was hesitant to make the overture. In private, he practiced different approaches but try as he might, he just couldn't find the right words to approach the subject of marriage. As time went on, growing weary of the situation, Juan finally mustered up enough courage to ask Carmen to marry him. He ultimately composed a flowery speech and memorized it for fear he'd stumble when the moment was upon him. Having devised a plan, he was becoming more confident and even went out on a limb and purchased what he thought was a diamond engagement ring. In Juan's world, it was expensive and although he really couldn't afford it, he reasoned it was worth it. The stone in the ring he thought was large enough to please Carmen and enough to tip the scales in his direction.

To celebrate their six-months of being together, Juan took Carmen to the *Nautilus* for a romantic dinner. The *Nautilus* was a high-end restaurant located on one of Key West's many piers. After dinner, Juan suggested they take a walk on the pier. When they were far enough from other strollers, Juan pointed to a wooden bench and they sat down. There was a full moon and a gentle breeze embraced them. Juan thought the mood was scripted for the occasion. Not wanting to lose the euphoria of the moment, or his nerve for that matter, he took her hand in his. Straightening his shoulders, Juan, fearing he'd stumble, blurted his canned proposal in a single breath.

"Carmen, you're the loveliest thing that's ever happened to me. I want to spend the rest of my life with you. Will you marry me?"

Juan reached in his pants pocket to retrieve the ring, but before he could produce it, Carmen jumped up and uttered in a mocking voice, "Marry you! Marry you! You must be crazy! You're the last person in the world I'd want to be married to."

Stunned, Juan rose from the bench and stammering, asked, "Wha...what?" A moment later, when Carmen's rejection hit him, he was instantly destroyed. His vision became blurred and he was suddenly swamped with the same feelings he had in high school when Lolita dumped him and his best friend betrayed him. It was all too much. Juan went berserk and grabbed Carmen by the neck with both hands, wrapping his fingers around her slender throat. When he began to squeeze, her eyes bulged, and she struggled with all her might. Her windpipe was constricted, and she couldn't scream. She pounded his chest with her fists and kicked at his legs. The harder she struggled the tighter he gripped her. When she finally went limp, he unceremoniously pushed her backwards over the pier railing into the wave-swept ocean below.

• • •

On the drive home and with his rage having subsided somewhat, he realized what he had done. He was so distraught, he secluded himself in his apartment for several days without food or sleep and paced the floor crying over his lost love. When he finally pulled himself together enough to read the newspaper, the article concerning Carmen's death caught his eye. It read:

> **The authorities announced earlier today they have identified the body that washed ashore Saturday morning as that of Carmen Ochoa, a secretary for a local insurance agency. An autopsy revealed that Ochoa had been strangled before being dumped into the ocean.**
>
> **Crime Stoppers is offering up to a $5,000 reward for information leading to the arrest and conviction of the person responsible for her death. The public is encouraged to contact the Key West Police Department or the Monroe County Sheriff's Office with any information regarding the case. They emphasize that absolute anonymity is guaranteed.**

Juan read and reread the newspaper account of Carmen's death. Although not named, Juan began to look at himself as a celebrity. In high school he was a nobody. In his diminished state of mind, he convinced himself he was a modern-day Don Quixote. Quixote was a fictional character of Spanish descent in a book his mother had read to him many years before. The hero of the story killed windmills which he thought were evil giants. Juan rationalized his mission was to rid the world of Jezebels, as much a blight on society as the evil giants Quixote faced. He immediately clipped the article and pinned it to his wall.

• • •

Feeling better having justified the kill, Juan returned to work. One afternoon as he was delivering a crate of fresh fish to a local restaurant, he happened to notice one of the waitresses. She could've been Carmen's twin sister they looked so much alike. Upon seeing Carmen's lookalike, Juan felt panicked as an unfamiliar force gripped him from within. All he could do was stare at the waitress. When the chef handed him the receipt for the fish delivery, Juan barely noticed and crammed the paper into his pants pocket.

"You okay, buddy?" the chef asked. "You look like you've seen a ghost."

Juan didn't reply. Feeling sick, Juan pushed the chef aside and made his way to the men's room. There he splashed cold water on his face and patted it dry with paper towels. He knew what he had to do. He turned to leave the men's room, and as he approached the door, he noticed a security guard's uniform hanging on a hook on the back of the door. *This may come in handy*, he thought. He scanned the rest room and ensured it was empty. Juan then quickly folded the uniform and tucking it into a plastic bag he removed from the trashcan, immediately left the restaurant.

Juan drove the delivery truck back to the fish distributor where he retrieved his vehicle. He stashed the bag containing the stolen uniform under the passenger seat of his car and headed back to the restaurant. He parked his car in an obscure spot in the parking lot and waited for the Carmen lookalike to emerge. About 3:30 p.m. she left the restaurant with a couple of other women. They were laughing and chatting, and when they approached the parking lot, they split up.

"See you tomorrow, Marlene," one of the women called out as they separated. His target, Marlene, was clad in a diving suit.

Juan watched as Marlene proceeded to a VW Bug parked on the back row of the parking lot. He waited for her car to pass in front of him. When it did so, he noticed the back seat of the Bug was bulging with scuba gear. Having grown up in Havana near the ocean, Juan was a skilled diver. *This may be easier than I thought.*

Juan followed Marlene to a popular diving spot and watched her remove flippers and scuba equipment from her car and head for the surf.

Armed with this information, Juan drove home. *If she has a set routine, our paths will cross again next Tuesday. That's when I'll introduce her to the hazards of scuba diving.*

. . .

The following Tuesday, just as Juan predicted, Marlene drove into the scuba shack's parking lot. Juan, now clad in his diving suit, exited his vehicle, and removed his diving gear from the trunk. He followed Marlene across the sand to the surf staying a safe distance away so as not to arouse her suspicion. He watched as she pulled on a pair of flippers and placed an air regulator into her mouth. When she wadded into the ocean, Juan followed. But kept a distance so as not to alert her of his presence. He mimicked her every move.

When he was sure they were far enough away from other divers, he closed the space between them, and from behind, he roughly jerked the regulator from her mouth. She was instantly engulfed in a cloud of bubbles as air continued to be emitted from the regulator. Apparently, in a panic she flailed her arms and wildly kicked her legs. Juan held the regulator far enough away so that she couldn't grasp it. He also had a tight grip on her ankle preventing her from surfacing. Although she was strong, Juan had the advantage—he had oxygen, she didn't.

Juan, having been around water most his life, knew that drowning was a form of suffocation. The lungs gradually fill with water making breathing oxygen impossible. Within four and six minutes of being cut off from oxygen, the body shuts down. Juan continued to subdue Marlene and after a few minutes, when her struggles subsided, Juan knew she was dead. Before releasing her, he removed a colorful clip from her hair and tucked it into his diving belt as a souvenir. He then swam to shore, stored his diving gear in the trunk of his car, and drove to his apartment.

Much to Juan's delight, the newspaper carried the story of Marlene's drowning the next day.

Authorities have identified a second woman's body that washed ashore yesterday as that of Marlene Chambers. Accidental drowning has been ruled out, but authorities are withholding details pending further investigation. However, this reporter has learned, because the MO is similar to that of Carmen Ochoa, whose body was discovered two weeks ago, police suspect a serial killer is on the loose and is victimizing local residents. Once again, the authorities request that if the public has information concerning either of the incidents, to contact them immediately.

As a reminder, Crime Stoppers is offering up to a $5,000 reward for information leading to the arrest and conviction of a possible killer and guarantees your anonymity. Again, anyone with any information that might aid the authorities in the investigation are encouraged to contact the Key West Police Department or the Monroe County Sheriff's Office.

• • •

Having deftly eliminated two Jezebels, Juan is encouraged in the belief that he is on a chosen path preordained by the Almighty to preserve and cleanse the female of the species. He thereupon begins to search for number three. It doesn't take long for him to zero in on another raven-haired beauty.

• • •

Elena Alvarez, owner of a hair salon on Marlin Street, downtown Key West, is just opening her beauty salon for the day. Juan passes it daily on his way to work. However, this particular morning Elena is late opening, and as she fumbles trying to balance an armload of supplies, she drops her keys onto the pavement. When she stoops to retrieve them, her long, dark hair sweeps around her face obscuring her features. It was at that moment Juan drives past the salon. Carmen! Dumbstruck, he's sure he's just seen Carmen's ghost, so he circles the block. By the time he comes back around, Carmen's lookalike is already inside the salon. A sign in the window of *The Cutting Edge* invites walk-ins. Juan parks his vehicle on the opposite side of the street and walks to the salon. When he enters, it looks as though the targeted stylist has just finished setting up her station, and after tying her apron around her waist, she retrieves her cellphone from the counter and slips it into her apron pocket.

"Good morning, my name is Elana. How can I help you?" Carmen's lookalike asks as she spots Juan.

Juan brushes at the hair above his ears, "Getting a little bushy," he says. "How 'bout a quick trim?"

"Yes, sir, just had a cancelation," Elana replies and motions for Juan to take a seat in her chair.

As Elana trims his hair, they chat about the weather and the economic situation. Juan learns from the name on the stylist's business license on display in a frame on her station that her name is Elana Alverez. Elana chats as she trims Juan's hair.

He learns that she works from 8:00 a.m. to 5:00 p.m.; lives with two roommates in an apartment not too far from downtown Key West; and takes the ferry to Miami every third Wednesday of the month to replenish her inventory. When asked why she doesn't buy locally, she explains that the supply house in Miami runs specials on the third Wednesday of the month and she saves a lot of money by taking advantage of the sales which are passed on to her customers. Armed with all the information he needs, Juan gives Elana a generous tip then proceeds to work.

Today is the third Monday of the month. When Juan arrives at work, he immediately requests the following Wednesday off, saying he has some business matters to attend to. Rusty Dougan, the owner and operator of the fish distributorship, likes Juan. Juan is a hard worker and never complains so Rusty grants Juan's request for a day off without question.

• • •

On Wednesday, Juan is in line early to purchase a ticket on the *Key Express*, the ferry that makes a daily run from Key West to Miami. It leaves Key West at 8:00 a.m. and starts the return trip from Miami at 5:00 p.m. arriving back in Key West around 8:00 p.m. The ferry has space to transport automobiles on the lower deck and the upper two decks are designed to accommodate passengers. Once aboard, Juan takes a seat on the third level where he can watch other passengers come aboard. His heart begins to race when he sees Elana standing in line to purchase a ticket. Once aboard, she takes a seat on the third level a few rows in front of him. He doesn't want her to see him, so he ducks behind the newspaper he brought with him.

· · ·

When the ferry docks in Miami, Juan stays back while the other passengers disembark. When he's sure Elana is off the boat he goes ashore. He isn't interested in where she's going so, he takes a bus downtown and spends the afternoon at a movie theatre. After the movie, Juan grabs a quick lunch at a nearby restaurant.

By the time he's finished, it's time to head back. He wants to be on board before the other passengers converge on the ferry. He takes the same seat so he can observe the surrounding area and soon spots Elana come aboard carrying two shopping bags. He watches as she places the bags into the bulkhead above the seat she'd occupied before.

Juan is now addicted to the notoriety he's been receiving from the media and wants victim number three's body to wash up in the Key West area in order to add to his serial killer status. He waits in his seat for the ferry to enter the waters surrounding Key West before approaching Elana. The sun is setting, and it's rapidly growing dark as the ferry skirts along the Florida Keys headed for its destination.

When the ferry is approximately 30 minutes from docking, Juan walks up the aisle pretending to be stretching his legs. When he approaches Elana, he stops.

"Well, hello!" he says. "So, we meet again."

Elana looks up, and recognizing Juan as one of her customers, smiles. "What are you doing here?"

Juan assumes a casual stance as he answers, "Had some business in Miami. I find taking the ferry is less stressful than driving."

"I agree. I really don't like the Overseas Bridge, it scares me."

Remembering his first crossing, Juan nods. "I'm stretching my legs. Want to join me?"

Elana looks around. Most of the other passengers are snoozing or reading the evening edition of the newspaper. No one seems to be paying much attention to them. "Sure, why not," she says, and rising from her seat, she grimaces, "You're right, my legs are cramped from sitting so long."

"Let's go up to the top deck and get some fresh

air and watch the sun set," Juan suggests. It is then he notices a gold cross suspended around Elana's neck. It is highlighted by the setting sun and sparkles in the last glow of day. When she bends to retrieve her purse from under her seat, the cross flips over and Juan detects the initials EA inscribed on the reverse side. They're barely visible probably eroded from years of wear.

"Okay," Elana replies, "I'm ready," and she follows Juan.

As they make their way up the stairs to the top deck, Juan says, "I like to stand in the back where it's more private."

Apparently thinking Juan is coming on to her, Elana hesitates. "I don't know, it's getting pretty chilly." Elana then turns back toward the stairs. Juan grabs her wrist. "What are you doing?" she blurts.

Since the two are the only ones on the top deck, and Juan knowing the noise of the engines will drown out any screams, he intensifies his grip on her and jerks her toward the stern of the boat.

"Let go of me!" Elana demands, struggling to free herself from his grasp.

"Oh, I will," Juan snarls, and forces her toward the stern. "You bet I will."

Elana still struggling to free herself from the grip Juan has on her wrist, starts to scream. Juan pins her against the railing and yanks the gold cross from her neck. Then in one swift motion, he flings her over the side into the churning foam created by the boat's forward movement.

Chapter Three

Attila

We're lucky enough to get through our first year in the Keys without experiencing a hurricane. We do get some high winds from time to time from the storms that move beyond us, but nothing as serious as a hurricane.

• • •

Mitch rents hanger space and keeps the Piper stored at Casey's airfield and at least once a week we take 'er up for a spin. Having just this past year been exposed to flying on a regular basis, I can see why Mitch is addicted and I, too, look forward to our excursions into the wild blue. Viewing the island chain from the air is exhilarating. When we fly above our neighborhood, I can pick out our house. On one occasion, much to my amazement, Mitch landed the plane on a strip of sand right in front of our house. He explained to me that the sand between the high and low water marks is usually solid enough for small planes to land. He also explained the reason for landing so close to our house was that he had had too much iced tea at lunch and needed to make a pit stop.

One afternoon as we're soaring through space, Mitch asks, "How'd you like to learn to fly?"

I take a moment to think about it and finally reply, "Humm, I like our present arrangement. After watching you maneuver all the instruments and gadgets, don't know if I'd have the temperament to actually fly the plane."

"You may just be surprised, so don't sell yourself short. If you change your mind…"

• • •

At the end of the year, when we transfer the last payment on the Piper back into our savings account, we celebrate at *The Sand Dollar.* Over frosty mugs of cold beer and jumbo shrimp cocktails, Mitch asks, "What's the point of living by the sea if we can't take advantage of it?"

Having previously considered that myself, I think for a moment and say, "Are you suggesting we buy a boat?" Mitch shoots me a smile that melts my reserve and the next day we add a modest cabin cruiser to our ever-growing inventory of expensive toys. We, of course, christen the boat *Teddy* to commemorate Mitch's tour on the USS *Theodore Roosevelt.*

Mitch painstakingly repaired the wooden pier that had been damaged by storm after storm and made it sturdy enough to dock the boat. And with the purchase of a cruiser, we put having a baby off for still another year.

• • •

Having acquired the necessities of life, a home, a plane, and a boat, we settle into a comfortable routine. I'm an early riser and enjoy taking a run up the beach before Mitch even stirs. The mornings are peaceful and the sun rising over the Atlantic is breathtaking.

The beach where I run is maintained by the subdivision's HOA and is usually kept free of debris other than seaweed and shells that wash ashore. This morning I'm surprised to see what looks like a large bag of trash undulating in the surf. As I get closer, I recognize what I thought was a bag of trash to be a human body. *Oh my God, someone drowned.* I don't take time to inspect the body but turn and race home as fast as I can.

In a panic, I burst into the bedroom and blurt, "Mitch, Mitch, someone has drowned up there!" and point toward where I saw the body.

"What, what?" Mitch groans as he sits up rubbing sleep from his eyes. "What's that about a body?"

When I explain in short breathless sentences about finding a body on the beach, Mitch is immediately out of bed pulling on his kaki cargo shorts and T-shirt. He grabs the phone on the nightstand, "I'm calling nine eleven," he says as he dials.

Mitch is on speaker phone and I hear the conversation. After going through the preliminaries, the 911 operator tells Mitch she's going to connect him to the detective unit. *The detective unit?*

"Detective Connors, how can I assist you?" a voice booms over the speaker interrupting my thoughts.

Mitch explains my having found a body on the beach, after which Connors informs him that a unit will be on the scene within the next half hour and for us not to touch anything relating to the body and to wait for the officers to arrive. At the time that struck me as being odd since it was obviously an accidental drowning.

Reverting to military language, Mitch replies, "Roger that," and hangs up.

"Detectives? I thought they'd send a rescue unit," I say.

"Don't know, with the bodies of a couple of unexplained deaths washing ashore just recently, they may suspect the one you discovered to be another victim," Mitch mumbles. A cold chill runs down my spine and I glance back over my shoulder in the direction of where I found the body. *Could it be?*

Just as promised, Detective Connors and another officer arrive within thirty minutes. We greet them on the front porch.

"I'm Mitchel McElroy," and pointing to me, Mitch says, "this is my wife, Samantha."

"Detective Liam Connors," Connors says. "I spoke with you earlier." Then pointing to the detective next to him, he says, "This is Detective James Lewis. Now, where's the body?"

Pointing up the beach, Mitch motions as he says, "It's up there. Samantha discovered the body this morning while running on the beach."

Connors looks in the direction Mitch is pointing. "Show us," he says.

As Mitch and I accompany the detectives up the beach, Connors asks, "Did you touch anything?"

Mitch looks at me. I answer, "No! From the distance, I first thought it was a bag of trash that floated up onto the beach, but when I got closer and determined it was a body, I ran home. Mitch called nine eleven as soon as I told him about finding a body that apparently washed ashore sometime during the night."

The four of us proceed up the beach. It's full daylight by the time we reach the body, and the details are apparent. It's a woman and she's on her back. She looks young. Her eyes are closed, and her long dark hair floats in the surf. She's clad in a floral sundress. It looks as though the fish had gotten to her before she washed ashore, and I have to turn away.

Upon seeing the body, Connors uses his cellphone to call it in, "Send the meat wagon. Looks like we've got another one."

I was stunned at his lack of respect. He must've noticed my expression. "Sorry, Mrs. McElroy."

I nod and start back to the house, Mitch joins me. We sit on the porch and watch. There's a lot of activity around our property as several vehicles, including the *meat wagon*, converge on the scene. Curious neighbors gather outside their homes, whispering among themselves.

Hours later, after the last of the investigators have left the scene, Connors and Lewis reappear. Their cruiser is parked in our driveway.

"We're going to canvass the area to see if anyone saw or heard anything late yesterday or last night that might relate to the death. And we'll need Mrs. McElroy to come to the station to make a statement since she's the one who discovered the body."

Mitch says, "Of course, when do you want us to do that?"

"The sooner the better," Connors says. "Time

dims details."

"Sure. By the way," Mitch says, "we've been following the newspaper accounts of mysterious killings in the area. I couldn't help but overhear you say, 'Looks like we've got another one.' Does that mean—"

"Yes," Connors interrupts and looks at me with steely eyes. "Yes, ma'am. Your find is number three—it appears as though we have a serial killer on the loose." Jangling his car keys, Connors looks up the beach, and with a thoughtful expression, adds, "You may want to reconsider your early morning runs, especially alone."

• • •

An article by lead columnist, Jack Evans, appears in the *Key West Communiqué* that evening. It reads:

The body of a local business owner was found on Coral Beach this morning. The victim, Elana Alverez, had been in the water for approximately two days according to the medical examiner. Alverez owned and operated a hair salon on Marlin Street. She was reported missing by her employees on Thursday when she failed to show up for work.

Alverez' co-worker, Theresa Martin, said

that the last time she saw Alverez was Tuesday evening. Martin stated that Alverez told her she was going to take the ferry to Miami early the next day to replenish their beauty supplies. Martin stated it was unusual for Alverez not to show up for work. She said the salon was Alverez' whole life. When authorities interviewed Alverez' roommates, they both stated they hadn't seen Alverez since Tuesday evening but concluded she opted to stay a few days in Miami. When asked, they stated they didn't know of any romantic interests in Alverez' life, but said Alverez was a private person. They said if she was meeting someone, she most likely wouldn't have told them.

Although there weren't any immediate signs of violence, on the body, this reporter wonders if Alverez is victim #3 of what appears to be a local serial killer. A pattern emerges: Carmen Ochoa's body was found a month ago washed up on Coral Beach. An autopsy determined she had been strangled. Marlene Chambers' body was discovered two weeks later. She had been scuba diving. Her scuba equipment was still intact, but it was determined by the ME that she had inexplicably drowned. Elana Alverez, like the other two victims, it appears died under questionable circumstances.

This reporter sees an MO emerging. It appears the killer disposes of the bodies in the ocean close enough in to wash up on shore and be discovered. And another interesting observation is that all three women look alike. Their photographs are included on page two of this edition of the Key West Communiqué.

• • •

After reading the article and studying the photos of the victims, Mitch says, "Sam, with a serial killer on the loose and terrorizing the Keys, I'd prefer you take Connors' advice and not run alone on the beach until this manic is captured."

"What makes you think—?" I begin.

Mitch bristles and interrupts. "Did you see the photos of the victims in the paper? Don't you think they bear an uncanny resemblance to you?"

"I didn't notice," I say and take the paper from Mitch. After looking at the photos, I'm stunned at how much they look alike and how close we all resemble each other. "You're right," I say. Then after a pause, I add, "How 'bout getting a dog, a fierce one, to run with me?"

"Sure, that's a great plan!" Then after rolling his eyes, says, "Sam, don't you understand? This guy's playing for keeps and you seem to fit the mode. However, I wouldn't trust a dog to ward off a determined serial killer. The dogs I had as a kid would have just bravely barked and run away with their tails tucked between their legs rather than make contact."

"It's not fair that I have to change or even give up my lifestyle because I *might* be a target. It may take years to solve the case and capture the so-called serial killer. And besides, you know how the ocean currents are. Those women could very well have drowned or been dumped in the ocean many miles from here."

"I'm not willing to risk it," Mitch replies. "If I could run with you, I would. But ever since I blew out my knee years ago playing basketball, I've not been able to run very far. If anything happened to you, I'd never forgive myself."

"Oh, Mitch. You worry too much about what *might* happen." When I notice the hurt look on his face, I'm ashamed of my overreaction. I soften and add, "However, I'm willing to compromise."

"Yeah! And how's that?" By the tone of his voice, it's obvious, Mitch is still irritated by my stubbornness.

"We get a dog to run with me and I won't run unless it's full daylight."

"Not much of a compromise, but if you're determined, it's better than nothing," Mitch replies and shakes his head.

• • •

The next morning Mitch and I visit the rescue shelter. Mitch is in a foul mood and when the attendant asks what we're looking for, Mitch pounces, "A killer dog. A big, mean one!"

The attendant nods, and the look on his face says, "With you around, why would you need a killer dog?" Instead he motions for us to follow him into the kennel. We pass cages containing a variety of canines. At the end of the corridor, the attendant stops and calls out, "Strike!" Instantly, a large animal slams into the wire cage on the other side of where we're standing. Growling and snarling, he bares his teeth in a threatening manner. "Meet Attila," the attendant says. "He's a one-man dog. When his owner died he was so unmanageable, the heirs brought him to us."

Having regained our senses after being scared out of our wits by the dog's sudden outburst, Mitch studies the beast and asks, "What breed is he?"

"German Shepherd," the attendant replies, as he rubs the dog's snout, apparently to reassure him we're friendly. The dog licks the attendant's hand.

"Attila was trained to attack on the command of s-t-r-i-k-e." The attendant spells the word and looks at the dog. "He's smart but he hasn't learned how to spell yet. If you do decide to take Attila, be careful how and when you use that word. He has a Dr. Jekyll-Mr. Hyde personality—and only one loyalty."

Mitch studies the dog more closely. "Are German Shepherds the best watch dogs?" he asks.

"No. In my opinion, the best watch dogs are the Doberman Pinschers. However, German Shepherds are a close second. We don't have any pinschers at the present time."

Still studying Attila, Mitch asks, "How do you designate in dog speak who the dog is to be loyal to?"

"Age old answer, the one who feeds him. In your case, you could take turns putting the food down and he'll be loyal to both of you."

Mitch looks at me. I shrug. "Okay, then, we'll take him," Mitch says.

The attendant puts Attila on a leash and hands it to Mitch. Attila, now in a Dr. Jekyll mode, affectionally rubs against Mitch's legs and we all head to the front of the building. Attila sits patiently waiting as we complete the paperwork. When Mitch removes his wallet to pay the kennel fee, he hands me the leash and I take the dog and head for the front entrance. Mitch completes the transaction and joins me. It's all I can do to hold onto Attila. He's strong and could easily tear a person apart.

"Good luck," the attendant says as we depart.

After the scary beginning, I'm surprised that Attila is so well behaved. He walks along beside us without incident as we head for our vehicle. However, he's attentive and his ears perk up at every sound. When Mitch opens the back hatch on our SUV, Attila jumps in without being coaxed to do so. On the way home, I turn and watch him. He's apparently enjoying the ride and the views from the windows and wags his tail when I turn to peer at him.

Upon arriving home, we soon learn that Attila is an outside dog. When we invite him into the house, he pulls back and defiantly sits down on the patio.

"Guess we need to get you a doghouse," Mitch says and heads back to the car. Attila is close on his heels. Mitch looks back, "Okay, fella, come on. You can pick out your own house," I hear him say as he opens the passenger door. When Attila hesitates, Mitch pats the passenger seat, "It's okay, buddy, you can ride in the front when Sam's not with us."

An hour later the boys return. Attila playfully

runs around the yard as Mitch assembles the new doghouse. In their absence, I found a braided throw rug in the garage that I now place on the floor of the completed doghouse. With a comfy bed, food, and water readily available, Attila makes himself at home and is soon taking a midafternoon snooze.

"Looks like a good idea," Mitch says and yawns. "Think I'll do likewise."

Chapter Four

Cuatro

Even though his identity is still unknown, Juan finds he's enjoying the notoriety he's generating as he reads and rereads the newspaper articles about the bodies that washed ashore. For the first time in his life, he's being noticed. Why, he's even making the headlines.

Taped to the wall above Juan's writing table are three objects: a *diamond* ring dangling on a string, an ornate plastic hair clip, and a small gold cross suspended on a broken slender gold chain. These objects were collected from his victims as *souvenirs*. He liked to think of the area as his wall of fame. They remind him of his quest for revenge. Juan also meticulously clips the articles from the newspaper detailing his exploits and carefully tapes them to the wall beneath his souvenirs.

After reading the *Key West Communiqué's* latest installment of his crusade to rid the world of Jezebels, Juan labors over an ancient typewriter, composing a note. When he finishes his typing, Juan leans back and rereads the message.

Numbers uno, dos, and tres, are now history.
Cuatro, cinco, seis remain a mystery.
Siete, ocho, nueve, diez watch your back.
You'd be wise to prepare for another attack.

Pleased with the results and satisfied the typewritten note conveys its intended meaning, Juan addresses an envelope to Jack Evans, crime beat reporter at the *Key West Communiqué*. Careful not to leave any incriminating evidence on either the stationery or envelope such as fingerprints or saliva, Juan mails the note.

• • •

Seated in his cubicle at the *Communiqué*, Evans sorts through a stack of mail that has been accumulating. He suddenly stops when he reaches Juan's letter and slices it open. As soon as Evans reads the note, he contacts Detective Liam Connors at the PD. Connors and Evans are old friends having worked many cases together, and Connors asks Evans to bring the note to the police station. The two men sit in Connors' office dissecting the contents of the writing.

"The first thing I noticed was that the writer used two languages when he composed the note," Evans says. "My guess is he wants us to think his nationality is either Cuban or Mexican. Remember, this is the first hint that he's bilingual."

"Agreed," says Connors. "But that may be to throw us off the scent and maybe not. Frankly, at this point, we have nothing else to go on."

"Humm, maybe so. Most Spanish courses do teach beginners the Spanish alphabet and how to count. So, the composer may not be Cuban or Mexican at all."

Connors looks thoughtful. "Judging from the victims' close resemblance, it appears that the perp is taking revenge on women who remind him of someone. Maybe an old girlfriend or someone who shunned him or gave him the heave-ho!"

"I've been thinking the same thing myself," says Evans.

"I'll have my men canvass the areas where the women lived, worked or frequented and show the victims' photos around. Maybe someone will make the connection with the woman and our killer." After a pause Connors adds, "Are you planning to print the note?"

"Wanted to talk to you about that first. If you think printing it in the newspaper would compromise any leads you have, I'll respect your judgment and not print it. However, my thought is, since he sent the note to me instead of you, this nutcase wants recognition for his acts and will continue to bait us and maybe slip up," Evans says.

"Good observation. However, at this point, we have nothing concrete to go on," Connors says and after a pause, adds, "Since you've been up front with me, I'm going to let you in on what we have. However, it's not to be publicized just quite yet," Connors says and looks at Evans raising his brow. "Kapish?"

"I understand and honor all *off the record* remarks, as you well know," Evans says somewhat agitated. "Maybe working in tandem by sharing information, we can catch the killer."

"Right. Strictly off the record," Connors says, "the ME's report shows that all three bodies have bruising, and they were able to match some of the bruise marks. Ochoa had bruising on her throat, Chambers had bruising on her ankle, and Alverez had bruising on her wrist. All were about the same size." After a pause, Connors adds, "If you think publishing the killer's note will aid in his apprehension, you have my permission. Maybe that will smoke the weasel from his den."

Evans replies, "Even though it's early in the game, sooner or later the killer will do something stupid. If we give him enough rope and string him along, he may just hang himself."

"And we may just build his confidence and

false sense of security with what he could easily conclude to be ineptness. And if he thinks he's smarter than we are, which he apparently does, he may become emboldened and get careless." After a pause, Connors adds, "As my old commander used to say, *Ignorance often leads to overconfidence, and overconfidence to mistakes and mistakes to arrests resulting in convictions.*"

"Exactly. Look for the note in my article in tomorrow's paper," Evans says as he heads for the door.

• • •

When the *Key West Communiqué* hit the streets the next day, every phone at the police department was lit up. People wanted to know what the cops were doing to keep their city safe from the lunatic. Juan was one of the callers. The press secretary for the KWPD fielded the calls. She was instructed not to answer questions but to recite a prepared response. "Yes, sir (or ma'am) the police department has assigned a special unit to investigate the killings. Solving these crimes is our top priority. We're suggesting you travel in pairs and stay in after dark if at all possible. Avoid contact with strangers and be careful who you invite into your home. Thank you for your cooperation."

Juan gloats as he hangs up the phone. *Looks like*

they have no clue as to who the serial killer is! I'll always stay one step ahead.

Not wanting to let his fame cool down, he immediately began searching for *cuatro*, number four. It was Saturday morning and Juan reasoned that many women would be grocery shopping. He drove to a local supermarket and parked where he could see the entrance of the store. A variety of women came and went but none matched the Jezebel description he was looking for. He was about to give up and change locations when Samantha drove up. When Juan saw her exit the SUV, he sat up straighter and pulled the binoculars from beneath the front seat.

Hello, Cuatro!

Juan waited for his target to leave the market and followed her home. Pleased with his shrewdness at having so easily identified her residence, he decided he'd conduct a surveillance starting early Sunday to determine her routine. Since that was one of his days off work, he wouldn't create suspicion—at least not at work.

Before dawn on Sunday the following day, Juan rose in excited expectation, and without taking time to eat breakfast, left his apartment. He drove to the street adjacent his target's home and parked near a grove of shrubs. He exited his car and found a secluded spot where he could watch the residence without being observed. He didn't have long to wait before his target emerged in a jogging suit. He watched as she performed a series of stretches and then turned, apparently calling to a dog. The dog immediately perked up and scampered over to where she was waiting. Together she and the eager animal started sprinting down the beach.

Juan knew the street where he was parked paralleled the beach. He hurriedly retrieved his vehicle and drove further up the street. He was clad in running shorts and tennis shoes and thought he would easily pass for a fellow runner who, coming from the other direction, he'd encounter her. Juan quickly parked the car and crossed the beach. Crouching close to the water, he waited. When he saw her coming, he started running toward her.

As Juan closed the distance between them, he took a rope from his rear pocket and gripped it tightly in both hands leaving just enough length between his grasp to wrap around his intended victim's neck.

• • •

When Attila begins to growl, I slow my pace and ask, "What is it, boy?" I'm suddenly frightened and look behind me half expecting someone to be there. No one is in sight, but I decide to head back anyway.

Before I can turn, a dark figure appears from nowhere and lunges at me. I instinctively shout "STRIKE!" When I do, Attila, growling and snarling, springs into action. As the runner and Attila collide, I'm thrown to the sand. Terrified, I watch Attila and the attacker scuffle around on the beach. Attila grabs an arm in his jaws, and clamping his teeth down, he violently shakes the attacker.

The attacker screams and tries to pull free. Attila hangs on for dear life. Apparently, in desperation, the attacker executes a flurry of kicks at the dog and finally lands a forceful blow to Attila's side. Attila howls in pain and loosens his grip on the attacker's arm, giving the attacker a chance to flee. Scrambling to his feet, the attacker races for the ocean and dives in.

I'm pretty shaken. Everything happens so fast, I'm still down after the attacker flees. I struggle to my feet, and as Attila barks and tries to give chase, I call for him to stop and retreat. He obeys and hobbles back to where I'm now standing. Although Attila drove the attacker off, I'm terrified and my first thought is to call Mitch. I reach into my rear pocket for my iPhone. When I pull it out, shards of glass slice my fingers. I must've landed on it when I fell and shattered the screen. With the loss of the use of my phone, I'm feeling more isolated than ever and have to fight the panic that is beginning to overwhelm me.

Attila whines and I look at him more closely and see pain in his eyes. "You're hurt and we need to get help. Let's get outta here." I shiver and take another quick look around. We then head toward home at a slow pace to accommodate Attila's injury. He can't run and even has trouble walking. I keep him close at my side and continue to keep watch over my shoulder in case the assailant decides to engage in a rematch.

• • •

Once home, I throw open the door and race in. "Mitch!" I cry. He must've heard the door slam against the wall. He's running down the hallway toward me and I fall into his arms. "Someone tried to attack me on the beach… Attila scared him off," I blubber clinging to Mitch.

"Are you hurt?" Mitch asks and pushes me back examining my face.

"No, I'm not. But Attila may be. He's on the patio. The attacker kicked him pretty hard in the side."

"You sure you're not—"

"Only shaken," I reply.

"Okay, I'll go see to him. Will you be—"

"Just shaken. I'm going with you," I say.

When we approach Attila, he's panting and lying just outside his doghouse. He whines when he sees us, and with great effort, attempts to rise.

"How ya doin', buddy?" Mitch asks, and kneels beside the dog. Attila makes a feeble attempt to wag his tail. Looking up at me, Mitch says, "He's apparently in a lot of pain. I'm, ah, that is we're, taking him in. There's an emergency weekend vet on duty in town and we need to get Attila there right away. I'll call Connors from the vet's office."

. . .

Dr. Fisher, the vet on duty, is standing at the counter talking to the receptionist when we enter. He takes one look at us and must've seen the anguish on our faces. Pointing to an examination room, he says, "Take him in there."

Mitch carefully carries Attila into the designated room and places him on a steel examination table. Attila looks at us with pitiful eyes and whines again. I want to cry.

"You stay with Attila," Mitch says. "I'm going out there," Mitch says and points to the waiting room, "and call Connors."

I nod.

Dr. Fisher meticulously examines Attila. Running his hands along the dog's side, Dr. Fisher looks up at me. "He has some broken ribs but doesn't seem to be hurt otherwise. How'd this happen?"

Not wanting to explain the circumstances, I say, "A stranger kicked him. What's the procedure for canine broken ribs?" I ask.

Dr. Fisher straightens up and drapes his stethoscope around his neck. "We'll have to splint him. You will need to keep him as still as possible, otherwise he could puncture a lung."

I look down at Attila, "Will you have to keep him overnight?" I ask anxiously.

"Not necessarily, that is unless you want us to." Attila whines again, probably rejecting the thought of an overnight hospital stay. "I think he'd be more at ease in familiar surroundings," Dr. Fisher says.

"I agree!" I say.

Dr. Fisher gives Attila an injection, "This'll keep him calm while I work on him." I rub Attila's head and coo to him as the vet applies the splint. "I'll send some pain inhibitors home with you. He may need them today. When you get him home, let him decide how he wants to position himself—that is sit up or lie down, however he will be the most comfortable."

Just as Dr. Fisher is putting the finishing touches on the splint, Mitch reenters the room. "What's the prognosis?" Mitch asks with concern in his voice.

"Broken ribs," I say. "And you?"

Mitch affectionally rubs Attila's snout as he says, "Tell you on the way home. Connors is going to meet us there."

. . .

Detective Connors is sitting in his vehicle waiting for us when we pull into our driveway. He joins us and watches as we make Attila comfortable. Attila must've understood the vet when Dr. Fisher said let him call the shots. However, he still stubbornly refuses to follow us into the house. He obviously prefers his doghouse and the braided rug. Almost as soon as Attila enters his domain, he's fast asleep.

"The tranquilizer must still be having some effect on him," I say to Mitch.

"He looks peaceful," Mitch replies as the three of us go into the house.

. . .

Once inside, I sit where I can keep an eye on the doghouse. Detective Connors sits at the kitchen table opposite me. "Did you get a good look at the assailant?" Connors asks as he peers over his reading glasses and grabs a pen and small tablet from his shirt pocket.

"No, not really. Everything happened so fast..." I reply.

Connors nods. "Even if you didn't see his

features, can you describe his build, hair color, anything that might help identify him?"

I try to relive the incident in my mind. "I'm thinking he was taller than me. I saw him racing toward me holding a rope in both hands out in front of him. The rope was at my eye level, so he must've been at least half a head taller than me. I think the rope was meant for my neck. It seems that he was exceptionally strong. He was able to shake a sixty-pound dog around when Attila clamped his teeth onto his arm. We just came from the vet, that's how I know how much Attila weighs."

Connors holds up a hand stopping me. "Has Attila had anything to eat or drink since the incident?"

"Yes!" Mitch interjects. "When we brought him home, he lapped up a generous amount of water from his dish…why do you ask?"

"I thought maybe we could get a sample of DNA from Attila's mouth and teeth. But it's obviously been digested," Connors replies.

"Oh!" Mitch says and shrugs.

"Even if we could, that would be a longshot at best," Connors remarks. Then looking back at me, he says, "I'm just grasping at straws. Go on."

I pause trying to remember details. "He cursed at Attila in both English and Spanish. From the sound of his voice, I didn't get the impression he was too old. Maybe late twenties or early thirties—certainly not sixties or seventies. He had on dark clothing, but I remember his tennis shoes were white. I had been knocked to the ground, and as he scuffled with Attila, I was close enough to notice there was a smear of what appeared to be red paint across the top of one of his shoes. I believe it was his left shoe. Don't ask me why I remember something that detailed, but I do."

Connors looks up from his note taking. "You have a remarkable memory. Most traumatized victims can barely remember their own name. The red paint smear detail may come in handy when we catch him." Then studying his note pad, he asks, "Anything else?"

"Not that I... Yes, there is one more thing. I remember him calling Attila by name." Mitch snaps his head up. "He must've been stalking us!" he blurts and looks out toward the street. "Son-of-a-bitch!"

Connors asks me, "Sure you didn't say the dog's name?"

"Yes, I'm sure," I reply. "The only thing I had time to say to Attila was STRIKE!" Fortunately, we were already inside the house and out of the earshot of Attila. Otherwise, Connors would be fighting for his life.

Chapter Five

Revenge

$H$is arm hurt like hell where the dog had sunk his teeth. However, Juan was able to swim in the shallows back to where he had parked. When he reached the spot he recognized, he stumbled out of the surf, weak from the excursion and encounter with the dog, and was barely able to make it across the beach to his vehicle. Opening the door, he fell onto the driver's seat and sat a few minutes catching his breath as he cradled his injured arm before engaging the ignition.

Back in his apartment, Juan took off his wet clothes and then poured a generous amount of hydrogen peroxide over the bite marks. Exhausted from his failed attempt to add another victim to his wall of honor, at least for now, he collapsed onto his bed and was soon fast asleep.

Restless, he tossed and turned. His dreams were haunted by the screams of the terrified women he killed. Somewhere in the recesses of his mind, he justified the murders by reminding himself they were Jezebels, all of them, and they and others like them deserved to die.

●●●

Morning found Juan refreshed and guiltless. He examined the wounds on his arm and surmised there was no infection present. That was good! He didn't want to have to explain to some doctor what had occurred. He remembered one afternoon, as he was helping unload the catch, the fishermen talking. Juan didn't know what initiated the conversation, he only heard one of the crew members telling the others: *…salt has antibacterial properties. It helps kill bacteria by osmosis.* Upon remembering this, Juan reasoned that the swim in the salt water was enough to help prevent infection.

Ravenous from the exertion the night before, Juan ate a hardly breakfast and dressed for work. He usually wore the company-issued short-sleeved T-shirt advertising Dougan's Fish Distributors. He liked that it was tight-fitting and showed off his muscular build. However, even though the day was hot and muggy, Juan donned a long-sleeved knit shirt to hide the bite marks on his arm. As he drove to work, he promised himself he'd get even with Cuatro and her attack dog. For most of the day at work, Juan mulled over his plan for revenge. He knew where Cuatro lived and her basic routine. Maybe she won the first round, but the fight had just begun, and he would be inflicting the devastating knockout punch when she least expected it.

When Juan returned home that evening, he again sat down at the antiquated typewriter. He was becoming distressed that his fame was waning and needed to remind the public and maybe himself that he was still alive and well. His message was short and sweet:

> *Cuatro,* **you may have foiled plan number one, but rest assured, the best is yet to come.**

Satisfied his note would cause the stir he was seeking, Juan painstakingly placed it in the envelope, upon which he had already typed the address, and again careful not to leave any incriminating evidence, such as fingerprints or DNA on the paper or envelope, he mailed it to Jack Evans at *Key West Communiqué.*

• • •

Upon receiving the envelope, Evans realized what it was because it closely resembled the first note. Not wanting to disturb any evidence, Evans didn't open it. Instead, he immediately contacted Connors and arranged to meet him at the police forensic lab.

Evans and Connors stood around a table in the lab and watched as one of the technicians meticulously sliced the flap on the envelope open with an exacto knife. With latex gloved hands, the tech extracted the note with a pair of tweezers and gently spread it open on the tabletop.

"Humm, looks like the same typewriter," Connors says as he examines the note. "See how the letter e is blurred."

"Yes, I noticed that on the first note. They must've been written on an old manual typewriter. I can tell because of the difference in the depth of ink deposited on the paper. The e is pretty light probably worn from years of use," Evans says, and Connors looks at him and raises his brow.

"I'm not a genius," Evans says and smiles. "Even in the news business, it took me a while to launch myself into the electronic age. Had trouble disciplining myself on how to learn to operate a computer. I used my trusty Underwood for many years so I'm familiar with the reluctance of many of us to shed the old ways of doing things in favor of the new. The vowel keys are always the first to show wear because of their frequent use."

The technician nods and says with a broad smile, "I concur with Mr. Evans' learned assumption that the notes were written on a vintage manual typewriter. We'll do testing on the envelope and notepaper and get back to you as soon as possible."

"Thanks, Stan," Connors says. "I don't hold out

any hope you'll find anything, but you never know. He's gotta slip up sometime. As my daddy always said, *Overconfidence breeds carelessness.*"

. . .

Back in Connors' office, Evans asks, "Who do you think *Cuatro*, or number four, is?"

"I know who she is!" Connors replies.

Evans frowns, "You do?"

"Got a call two days ago. *Cuatro* was assaulted on the beach not far from her residence while running along the shoreline. She had her dog with her, and the dog fought off the attacker." Connors rubs his chin, then adds, "She's a dead ringer for the first three victims. Name's Samantha McElroy."

"Holy Mother of God! I know the McElroys. Met them at Casey's airfield. Our paths cross sometimes when we go flying. Mitch is ex-Navy and a damn good pilot." After a pause, Evans asks, "How do you want the newspaper to handle the recent note? Publish or not?"

"Not sure. It's apparent the killer is seeking publicity. After all, it's been two weeks since his last kill and claim to fame."

"What worries me is the best is yet to come comment. He seems determined to carry out his diabolical plan," Evans replies. "Is your department providing protection for Mrs. McElroy?"

"Absolutely! We have a team on the job twenty-four seven. However, she insists on her daily run on the beach. Says it's the only way she gets exercise and fresh air. Her argument is it may take months or even years to catch the killer, and by that time she says she'll *be old and fat*— her words, not mine."

Evans interjects, "What's that old saying, *vanity kills*?"

"Humph! So do serial killers," Connors grunts. "I've assigned one of our more athletic officers to run with her. But she's declined the offer." Connors, looking disgusted, adds, "McElroy's pretty stubborn. You'd think after her dog was almost killed, she'd be less inclined to run on *that* beach."

"You briefly mentioned the dog, what happened?" Evans asks.

"When Samantha McElroy was attacked, Attila, the family pet, as I stated, fought the attacker off and chased him into the ocean. Attila received a couple of broken ribs in the scuffle. It's going to take a while for the dog to recover."

"Attila? Like in Attila the Hun? Hold on, let me guess, he's a German Shepherd, right?" Evans asks. "You're one smart hombre! Why haven't you won the *Pulitzer* yet?" Connors asks sarcastically.

"*Yet* is the operative word here, and I'm working on it so give me a break. I'm only thirty-two years old, you know," Evans shoots back. "There's always next year…or the year after!"

"No, I didn't know you were still a neophyte. You've had us all fooled. Besides, what's age got to do with anything anyway? And since you brought it up, Harper Lee was only thirty-one when she won the *Pulitzer* for *To Kill a Mockingbird*," Connors says.

"Didn't know you were so well read, I'm impressed," says Evans.

"Hell, man, I got talents you never heard of." Evans rolls his eyes, "In the meantime, do we print the note?"

Connors takes a moment before answering. He finally says, "If we print it, the killer gets what he wants, namely notoriety. If we don't, he may become more assertive in order to generate more news to achieve that infamous status. What's your take?"

"In light of what you suspect, I say we print it. If printing it satisfies him for the time being that may buy you guys time to figure out who he is," Evans says. "It's my opinion that, print it or not is immaterial to the ultimate outcome. It's obvious from his first note that he intends to keep killing." After a pause, he adds, "Maybe Dorinda will blow him away."

"Dorinda! Don't tell me we have another hurricane on the horizon!" Connors blurts. "I hadn't heard…"

"Not public yet, I got wind, pardon the pun, just as I was leaving the newsroom," Evans replies. "It'll probably be on the evening news."

Connors rubs his face with both hands. "That's just what we need. Our resources are already stretched to the breaking point—not to mention our patience."

"It's about time you guys earned your pay!" Evans teases. "As far as your patience, I don't think you ever had any." Both laugh.

Levity is something that escaped them for too long a period of time. With a serial killer on the loose, the police department was taking a lot of heat. With a certain segment of the public wanting to defund the police, Connors knew he and the rest of the department couldn't waste a lot of time. Fortunately, the department had the press on their side.

Chapter Six

Dorinda

When I hear a hurricane may be headed for Key West, I research storms on my computer. The website tells me that storms form over tropical or subtropical water. The winds must reach 74 miles an hour to classify the storm as a hurricane. There are five classes of hurricanes, one to five, depending on the maximum sustained winds. A category five, or Cat 5, hurricane is the most powerful and sustains winds above 155 miles per hour. To put it in perspective, large hurricanes release energy equivalent to that of atomic bombs. My research only adds to my consternation.

• • •

Mitch and I sit on the patio drinking our morning brew. When I search the sky, it's hard to believe a violent storm is in the offing. The day is sunny and a slight breeze ruffles the palm fronds. Attila is snoozing in a warm spot on the deck. He occasionally jerks his legs in a running motion. I wonder if he's dreaming of chasing killers or just rabbits.

Our police *babysitter* called this morning.

Because of the incoming storm, the department has suspended our onsite protection. The manpower is needed elsewhere. Not sure it's safe to go for my morning sprint without protection so I scan the morning paper and read one of the frontpage articles.

"Dorinda is the fourth hurricane to have formed in the Atlantic this season," I say to Mitch paraphrasing the information I gleaned from the article. "Guess we were lucky to have avoided the first three, but it looks like Dorinda is going to make up for it."

Mitch looks up and I notice concern in his eyes. "What else does the paper say?" he asks.

"Humm, National Hurricane Center says Dorinda's battered the Caribbean working her way in our direction. Puerto Rico, Dominican Republic, Bahamas, Turks and Caicos Islands were all hit. The average mean season produces as many as twelve named storms with only six turning into hurricanes." I learn more about hurricanes from the newspapers than I ever learned in high school, and to be honest, hurricanes scare the hell outta me.

"Only six! That's encouraging," Mitch replies. "If Dorinda is number four, we only have two more to sweat out."

"I think you missed the point. Only six out of twelve evolve into hurricanes. That doesn't mean the three before Dorinda were of hurricane status. So, we could have five more to go," I say.

"Thanks for pointing that out. I feel much better," Mitch mutters and rolls his eyes.

"We knew that when we moved here. We opted to take our chances with hurricanes instead of earthquakes. Remember?" I say and glare at Mitch.

"You're right," Mitch says reluctantly. Pointing to the newspaper, he asks, "Anything else?"

"Yes. However, it's not official yet but it looks like the island may have to evacuate to the north."

"Swell. What about us?" Mitch asks.

"The hurricane center estimates Dorinda will hit day after tomorrow unless she changes direction. The Overseas Highway is already jammed with traffic. Do you think we should be preparing to leave?"

"Don't know. According to Ray, our house is pretty sturdy. It's survived a lot of storms.

I don't want to fight with the traffic on the bridge if we don't have to. Crossing it, even in good weather, gives me the willies, not to mention the weight of all that traffic crossing at the same time…"

"Point made. If you think we'll be okay here, I'm willing to stay," I say, then add, "You appear to be out of sorts this morning. Are you all right?"

"Sorry, honey. Don't mean to be so grumpy.

I'm just nervous not knowing what to expect. Think I'll tour the property and make sure everything is battened down."

When Mitch rises, Attila must have heard the chair scrape against the patio deck. He awakens and joins Mitch. Attila's ribs seem to have healed and he's getting spryer by the day. As I watch them walk toward the front of the property, I notice Mitch has his hands jammed into his pants pockets. I recognize that to mean he's wrestling with making a decision.

I fold the newspaper and go into the house. I don't want to let on to Mitch, but I'm pretty worried about the hurricane myself. That, combined with a serial killer on the loose, has made even me edgy.

• • •

The fish distributor shut down operations at the end of the workday, pending the outcome of Dorinda. On his way home from work, Juan stops at a news vending machine and purchases the evening edition of the *Key West Communiqué*. Normally, he watches the news on TV unless he's expecting an article about his exploits. He gloats when he sees his current note to Jack Evans on the top half of the front page. The accompanying article reads:

> ***Apparently, killing three women in the prime of their lives is a joking matter to the***

killer. He continues to seek notoriety by sending cryptic notes to this reporter like the one printed below. The note addresses his perceived fourth victim who he calls Cautro:

Cuatro, you may have foiled plan number one, but rest assured, the best is yet to come.

When the note was turned over to Key West authorities, this reporter was told that Psycho-man had attacked still another woman, one he calls Cuatro, on the beach early Tuesday. Fortunately, the dog she had with her fought off the attacker and the woman escaped uninjured. She described her attacker as a bilingual male in his late twenties or early thirties, approximately 5'11" to 6' tall with medium length dark hair. He was wearing dark colored clothing and white tennis shoes.

The authorities reiterate the danger associated with Psycho-man and ask that you please take all necessary precautions to protect yourselves, especially women matching the descriptions of the first three victims whose photographs have appeared in previous editions of this newspaper and appear again on page 3 of this issue.

When Juan reads *Psycho-man*, the name given to him by the reporter, he becomes furious. In a rage, still standing by the newspaper stall, he tears the newspaper to shreds. Then realizing he destroyed the latest addition to his wall of fame, he purchases another newspaper and heads home. Brooding over the disrespect displayed on the front page of the *Communiqué* for all the world to see, he blames *Cuatro* for his woes, and reinforces his determination to even the score with that Jezebel.

• • •

"I read your latest on Psycho-man in last evening's edition," Connors says to Evans when they meet the next day in Connors' office. "Thanks for not mentioning the red paint smear on the shoe. That could be the nail that seals his fate and if he knows we know, he'll destroy the shoe."

"Thought you'd like to keep at least one ace up your sleeve," replies Evans.

"Good thinking on your part," Connors remarks. "I think the pseudonym, Psycho-man, is an apt description for this bastard, but you're sticking your neck out. He's worked pretty hard to build a reputation and I don't think he'll take the slam lightly."

"Precisely!" Evans agrees. "However, maybe I can smoke 'em out—and force him to take on someone his own size for a change."

"Don't know if I can let you do that. You're one of the citizens I'm sworn to protect…" Connors says.

"But I have an advantage," Evans counters.

"How's that?"

"I'll be expecting him. Consequently, he loses the element of surprise. And being in a state of rage to retaliate for the insult puts him at a greater disadvantage. He won't be thinking clearly. I'm no martyr, but if handle it right, we can end this charade before we lose another beauty," Evans says.

"You have a point, and I don't disagree with your strategy particularly since you've already set the wheels in motion. However, I'll have to insist that one of my men remain nearby day and night."

"Might scare 'em off," Evans replies.

"Chance I'm willing to take," says Connors. "We don't need to add you to the body count."

"Dorinda may take care of that," Evans says. "Our weatherman on staff at the newspaper reports she's headed straight for us. Probably make landfall day after tomorrow."

"Yep, I heard that. And to add to the equation, I've had to dispatch a couple of units to the bridge to help with the influx of traffic trying to get to the mainland," Connors remarks. "You plan on riding it out?"

"Yes. I've been through hurricanes before—"

"If this one remains a Cat 5," Connors interrupts, "sticking it out is tantamount to suicide in my book."

"I know…" Evans says. "Maybe Psycho-man will get careless and Dorinda will take care of him for us."

"We can always hope. Would save a lot more lives and the taxpayers a lot of dough," Connors remarks. "Just make sure *you* don't get careless and take unnecessary risks." After a brief pause, Connors adds, "It's Psycho-man's carelessness we're praying for!"

Chapter Seven

Oh, Hell!

Mitch and I keep an eye on the news and continue to follow the progression of Dorinda. We check and re-check the house and our hurricane supplies. We educate ourselves on what to expect as the hurricane closes in. Huddled together on the front porch of our home, we watch dark clouds gather as the winds pick up. From our vantage point, we can see waves frothing with white caps as they rush to shore and can hear the ocean's ferocious roar. Debris is flying everywhere, and Attila begins to whine as he moves closer to us. *Perhaps he'll change his mind and come into the house when things really become unrelenting.*

Mitch puts his arm around my shoulders, I don't know if it's to reassure me or him. I hope he's not thinking what I'm thinking—that we made the wrong decision and should've left the island when we had the chance.

"Come on, honey. Let's go inside and batten down the hatches," Mitch says.

I nod and we start toward the door. I notice Attila's ears perk up when, over the din of the storm, we hear what sounds like a woman screaming for help. Attila barks and prances around our legs, apparently also having heard the screams.

"Did you hear that?" I ask and look in the direction of the source.

"I did," Mitch replies. "Sounds like someone in distress." Attila follows Mitch as he walks to the edge of our lawn and looks down the street. "Oh, my God!" he shouts, and I follow his gaze. We see Renee Benjamin, one of our neighbors, running toward us. Renee's holding her three-year old daughter, Cindy, in her arms. Her demeanor, particularly the way she carries Cindy while scurrying down the street, makes it appear something serious has happened to Cindy.

Mitch and I run to meet Renee. We struggle against the wind and fight like crazy to get to her. She has the wind at her back making her progress easier. As Renee closes the gap, we can see blood coming from a deep gash on Cindy's forehead. Renee screams, "Please help! Cindy's badly hurt…" Renee is in a panic mode and clearly desperate.

When we come together, Mitch takes Cindy from Renee and does a cursory examination of the deep gash and assesses the degree of urgency "What happened?" he asks as we turn toward our house.

"Cin…Cindy…door blew open…Fluffy ran out.

Cindy…ran after the cat. Oh God, before I could get her back inside, she was struck by flying debris."

"We need to get her to a hospital ASAP," Mitch says. "Where's Chuck?"

Renee and Chuck Benjamin live just a few doors from us. They own the Ford dealership in Key West. And being civic-minded, Chuck is a member of the search and rescue squad and trained in first aid.

"Was called out. Don't know where…" Renee sobs. "He's not answering his cellphone."

• • •

With Renee and Cindy in tow, we fight through the wind and debris and make our way back to our house where Mitch makes several attempts to reach 911. We had heard earlier that most medical facilities were closed and employees were instructed to find a safe place to wait out the hurricane.

I know from my first aid training that scalp wounds bleed heavily because there are so many blood vessels close to the surface of the skin. I also know that applying compressions to the wound will slow the bleeding. I rush to the pantry and retrieve our first aid kit. When I return, Renee and I wipe the wound clean with a handful of tissues and fold strips of gauze and apply them to Cindy's wound. We're successful and finally get the bleeding stopped. However, when Cindy opens her eyes, she has an unusual, dazed look about her. I'm concerned she may have sustained a concussion or worse yet, brain damage.

"Can't get through to nine-one-one," Mitch says as he returns to the room. I gather up the blood-stained tissues and gauze and head for the kitchen motioning for Mitch to follow. Renee follows us with her eyes but stays at Cindy's side.

"What is it?" Mitch asks, as we sit down in the kitchen. Attila is cowering under the table. It appears the chaos surrounding the storm, Cindy's emergency, and being confined in the house all at the same time are too much for him and he's having trouble coping. He places his snout across the top of Mitch's shoes, apparently seeking protection and reassurance. Mitch scratches Attila's head to comfort him.

"Oh, Mitch. I think Cindy may have some brain damage, or at the very least, a concussion" I whisper. "When my best friend in grade school, Jessica Walters, was hit in the head with a swing during recess, she had a similar wound and was hospitalized with a concussion."

"Oh, no. We need to get her—"

"I know, but how?" I ask.

Mitch rubs the back of his neck. "That's a good question. Nine-one-one must be overwhelmed, no one answers. The medical facilities are shut down until the hurricane passes. The bridge is still jammed with traffic being diverted to the mainland, so that's not an option. We can't take the cruiser out in this weather, that would be suicide. That leaves the plane as our only choice."

"Oh, no! How can you fly in this?" I blurt remembering the enormous tidal waves and the dark, threatening sky.

"Although it looks ominous, it can be done under certain conditions. Since we're not yet in a full-blown hurricane, and the wind and weather are within legal and safe parameters, planes are allowed to take off. Once airborne, I can maneuver the plane into a safe path above the storm."

Trying to find a reason for Mitch not to fly, I say, "Even so, Miami is probably flooded with evacuees fleeing the hurricane. The hospitals are most likely swamped…"

"I agree, but I don't have to land in Miami. I can fly up the coast to Orlando. Orlando's far enough north not to have had an influx of evacuees and the hospitals there are large enough to have specialists available." After a pause, he adds, "Probably more on hand than usual in anticipation of injured evacuees."

Backed into a corner, I have no valid reason to object further. Besides, Cindy is in urgent need of medical attention. "What's next?" I ask.

"I've been thinking about that. As you know, the Piper only has two seats," Mitch says and looks at me with worry in his eyes.

I nod.

"That means only room for the pilot and one passenger," Mitch continues.

"I understand, Mitch. Renee must go, she can hold Cindy on her lap." After a moment, I add, "You need to get going before the weather gets worse."

"Roger that," he says in a subdued tone. "I need to grab a few things. Would you fill Renee in on the plan?"

"Yes, you get yourself ready."

"Mitch rises but pauses on his way to the bedroom. Looking back at me, he says, "This is a hard decision, Sam. With Psycho-man still out there…"

"He'd be a fool to be prowling about in this weather. Besides, I have Attila on my side." I say, sounding braver than I feel.

• • •

Standing in the open doorway, I watch Mitch with Renee still holding Cindy drive away heading for the airport. Before I can close the door, something furry brushes past my legs. It's Attila and my heart skips a beat when he bounds out the open door. I watch as he leaps from the porch and begins running after Mitch's vehicle. I rush out the door and race after him calling his name. He's so far ahead of me, it's apparent he doesn't hear me. The wind, rain, and flying debris finally force me to give up the chase. Wet and cold, I return inside.

The interior of the house is dark and gloomy as Mitch had closed the shutters earlier in the day. When I suddenly realize I'm now truly alone, an eerie feeling engulfs me. I try to get reception on the television and radio without success. I check my iPhone. The display tells me there's no service. The storm must've disabled the cellphone towers as well as shutting down the electricity. It seems everything has gone dead, everything that is except the raging storm.

• • •

When Mitch arrives at the airfield, he parks close to the hangers and runs inside. After opening the hanger door where the Piper is housed, he hurries back to the car and drives it inside the hanger. Before he can transfer Renee and Cindy into his plane, Casey appears from the rear of the hanger.

"Mitch! What in hell's name are you doing

running around in this weather?"

"Have an emergency, Casey. Need to get a child to a doctor ASAP." Mitch motions toward where Renee is still cradling Cindy in her arms. "Renee's daughter, Cindy, was hit by some flying debris and received a nasty gash on her head. Sam thinks she may have a concussion or maybe even brain damage. Since our medical facilities have shut down, I have no choice but to fly them to Orlando."

Casey glances out the open hanger door then back at Mitch. "Your Piper may not have enough horses to take that on," he says, nodding toward the wind and pounding rain which is apparent through the open doorway. Casey turns back to Mitch and tosses him the keys to his Cessna jet. No words are necessary. The look on each of their faces says it all. Mitch would later say Casey was a lifesaver. That told me it would have been a grave mistake to have ventured out in Mitch's Piper.

"Come on, Mitch, I'll drive you over to my hanger. You start 'er up and get acquainted with the flight deck. The charts are between the pilot and copilot's seats. I'll get your passengers aboard."

As Casey drives Mitch's car to an adjoining hanger, Mitch explains to Renee the change of plan. As soon as they stop, Mitch bounds up the stairs and boards the plane. Casey carries Cindy onto the plane followed by Renee. Casey lays Cindy across two seats and buckles a seatbelt around her. He motions for Renee to take the seat immediately across the aisle from where he placed Cindy. Once the passengers are secure in the cabin, Casey joins Mitch on the flight deck.

"Questions?" Casey asks.

"Looks similar to the ones I flew in the Navy, only on a smaller scale," Mitch replies without taking his eyes away from the control panel. "As soon as I get radio contact, I'll alert the control tower and FAA of my destination and the route I'm taking."

"Okay, you'd better get started. The safe-to-fly window is rapidly closing," Casey says.

"Roger that," Mitch replies. "And thanks, Casey. I'll bring 'er back unscathed."

"Know you will," says Casey, "just bring yourself back unscathed." He then exits the plane and waves over his shoulder.

Mitch raises the steps and secures the door behind Casey. Minutes later, he taxies out of the hanger, down the runway, and is soon soaring into a dark, menacing sky.

• • •

My anxiety increases with Attila running off and me having lost all contact with the outside world. Not knowing what to expect when Dorinda's full-blown wrath descends on Key West, I wrap in a blanket and huddle in the corner of the sofa. The sounds of the wind, rain, sea and flying debris are deafening, and I pray Mitch is safe somewhere up there.

Chapter Eight

Home Alone

Juan takes advantage of the fish distributorship having shut down to wait out the hurricane. This lull affords him time to surveil his intended target. From his previous blind spot, Juan sits in his car, and is able to spy on the McElroy's entire property. He's been there most of the morning and is getting inpatient. However, Juan doesn't fear the storm. He had been through a few when he lived in Cuba and knows when it's time to shelter.

It's late afternoon when Juan observes the man and woman exit the house and stand on the front porch. He perks up and grabs his binoculars in time to see the couple suddenly run from the porch and down the street in the opposite direction from where he's stationed. He also notices the damn dog is with them. Juan keeps watching and soon observes the couple return. The man is carrying a child who appears to be injured. Another woman is with them. She appears distressed and disoriented. They all disappear into the house, including the dog.

The storm is getting worse and Juan fears he'll have to abort his mission before too long and head home to hunker down until Dorinda passes. Besides, with extra people present in the house, there's no way he can pounce on his intended prey. Just as he's getting ready to leave, he sees the front door open and watches the man carry the child to a car. The man's followed by the other woman who appears to be still distressed. His unmistakable target stands in the doorway and waves as the others drive off. He watches the dog bolt from the house and chase after the car. He can scarcely believe his luck. It appears the Jezebel is now home alone with no vicious dog to protect her.

Little time to waste, Juan quickly retrieves the stolen security guard's uniform from under the passenger seat and squeezes into it. He then drives to within a short distance of the McElroy's residence. He exits his car and starts down the rain-swept street. When he's adjacent to the McElroy's residence, he approaches the front door and rings the doorbell.

• • •

I'm still curled up in the corner of the sofa huddled in the blanket when the doorbell rings. I immediately think it's Mitch returning, and I run to the door. However, I pause before opening it, and ask "Who is it?"

"Subdivision security," a male voice answers

from the other side of the door.

I look out the peephole in the door and see a man dressed in a security uniform. He has his back to me and is looking toward the street, apparently assessing the storm.

"What is it you want?" I ask.

"Security is conducting a welfare check on all of our residents. Are you okay in there?"

"I…I don't know. I think so," I answer.

"Would you let me make a quick pass through to check things out?" the male voice persists.

I'm suddenly cold with fear. "What would you be checking for?" I ask.

"Oh, making sure the gas connections are tight and that no electrical attachments have come lose which could cause a fire," the male voice replies.

Funny, I'd not heard of subdivision security before now. But we haven't been caught in a full-blown hurricane before either. Still apprehensive, I say, "I think—"

"It'll only take a minute, ma'am. It's my job…"

I look out the peephole again. He looks harmless enough, so I finally say "Okay," and release the deadbolt. I crack the door open, and when I glance down at his feet, I spot the red paint smear on his left tennis shoe. I gasp and he must've noticed the terrified look on my face as he instantly slams his shoulder against the door. I scream and push back with all my might. The stranger and I then engage in a tug-of-war pushing back and forth against the door. My adrenaline must have kicked in because my 126 pounds enable me to hold him off.

My strength is rapidly waning and waves of panic sweep over me. Then, suddenly out of nowhere, I hear a vicious growl and feel the door suddenly go slack. When that happens, I'm caught off balance and stagger as the door slams shut. Upon regaining my balance, I immediately lock the door. Through a small side window beside the door, I watch as Attila pounces on the stranger. Although they move from my sight, I can hear a combination of screams and growls fade into the windy, rainswept night.

My stomach churns, and when my knees buckle, I fall to the floor in the entrance way. Spent from fear and the exertion of pushing on the door to block entry, I bury my head in my hands and sob. After a few minutes, I hear a whining sound from the other side of the door. I know it's Attila but I'm too frightened to open the door for fear the stranger may also gain entry. Soon the whining is accompanied by scratching on the door. I can't ignore the fact that Attila saved my life once again, now he's asking for me to return the favor. If I leave him out there in the night, he'll certainly parish in the hurricane. I cautiously open the door partway. When I do, Attila squeezes through the slight opening and rubs against my legs. Poor thing. He's shivering and dripping wet. I secure the deadbolt then retrieve some towels from the linen closet and pat Attila dry. As I do, I look for injuries. He appears to be unharmed.

After drying Attila, I place the towels in the hamper and go to the bedroom. Attila follows close behind. I take Mitch's service weapon from the nightstand. Mitch cautioned me to always treat a gun, any gun, as though it were loaded. Mitch told me if we had a break in, we'd be dead before we could get the gun loaded so I know he keeps it loaded.

As I pass the pantry on my way to the kitchen, I remove a flashlight from our hurricane supplies and retrieve two bottles of water from the frig. I empty one into a bowl for Attila and take the other, along with the weapon and flashlight, to the living room and once again curl up in the blanket. Fear and exhaustion have taken their toll and I fall into a fitful sleep fraught with disturbing nightmares. With Attila beside me, I feel safe.

• • •

Juan had parked close to the McElroy's and

is able to ward off the charging Attila with a tree branch that had been dislodged during the storm allowing him to reach and enter his vehicle. He succeeds in clamoring onto the driver's seat while slamming the door in the dog's face. Once inside his car, he slouches behind the steering wheel, grateful to be out of the dog's reach. However, Attila doesn't give up easily. Barking and snarling, he jumps at the car door scratching at it with his claws. Juan is spent and knowing he's safe, ignores the dog. He accesses his injuries. His hands are covered with bites, but other than that, he seems to be okay. *Next time it'll be the dog seeking cover!*

Having reached the safety of his vehicle, and determining he was not seriously injured, Juan explodes in anger and pounds the steering wheel with his fists. *That Jezebel! She'll pay for this.* After a moment, and still in a rage, Juan slams his car into gear and speeds off. *Too bad that damn dog isn't in my path.* Through the torrent of rain, Juan makes his way to his apartment. The old hurt of his high school sweetheart dumping him for his best friend swirls in his brain and fuels his anger and his resolve to rid the world of evil women. The rain makes it difficult for him to see out of the windshield, but since there's no other traffic on the streets, he makes it home with relative ease.

. . .

I'm awakened by the sound of the television. Through a haze, my groggy brain realizes the power is back on. *Probably didn't turn the TV off when we lost power last night.* I watch as a news reporter drones:

> *...another miracle. Dorinda had a change of heart and before making land, she turned back out to sea and is headed north but far enough out in the Atlantic not to pose a threat to the Florida coastline. Although the islands suffered a great deal of damage and flooding from the violent wind and rain, we were spared the wrath of a Cat 5 hurricane and 155 mile per hour winds which would have destroyed much of the Keys.*

I can scarcely believe what I'm hearing. I run to the small window beside the door and look out. Many of our neighbors are milling about the debris-strewn neighborhood. I determine it's safe for me to join them. Attila whines as he paces the floor. He apparently needs to go out. I attach him to his leash, and we go out into the front yard. Once outside, I overhear conversations concerning how fortunate we were to have avoided the full impact of

Dorinda. I thank God for sparing us from the wrath of the hurricane and protecting me from Psycho-man. Just the thought of last night's encounter makes me shudder. After attending to his business, Attila is still edgy and struggles fiercely against his leash. He's probably remembering his run-in with Psycho-man as well. I pet his head in an attempt to reassure him that everything is going to be alright.

I'm concerned for Mitch's safety, so I go back inside intending to call him as well as Detective Connors. Unfortunately, I have a *no service* display on my iPhone and conclude the towers must still be down. Frustrated and restless, I wait for cellphone service to be restored. I'm confident Psycho-man won't return with all the neighbors in plain view and in close proximity, so I go back outside. I unleash Attila and busy myself by clearing some of the debris from our property. Attila, ever vigilant, stays close to me. As I empty trash into the dumpster, Detective Connors drives up. He exits his vehicle and walks to where I'm collecting the garden tools.

"Mornin' Mrs. McElroy," he says, and leaning down, pets Attila on the head.

I feel Attila stiffen, so I reassure him with a gentle, "It's okay, boy."

Not knowing how close he came to being a doggie dinner, Connors continues, "Apparently, you weathered the storm okay. Is Mr. McElroy home?"

"No, he isn't. We had an emergency arise and Mitch flew our neighbor and her daughter to Orlando. I was going to call him and you as soon as service was restored. I had another visit from Psycho-man last night," I say. "Thank God Attila was there to ward off the attempted attack. Psycho-man was wearing a uniform representing himself to be HOA security."

"Oh, my God! Are you all right?"

I nod.

"I wouldn't have thought he'd be out in the midst of the storm," Connors says scratching his head.

"Me neither but he was." I invite Connors inside, and as I make a pot of coffee, I began to tell him what happened, including the reason for Mitch's trip to Orlando. About half-way through my narration, the phone rings. Mitch! I eagerly grab the phone grateful it's now working. "Hello!" I yell much louder than intended.

"Sam, are you all right?" Mitch asks with concern in his voice.

I'm so overcome with emotion upon hearing Mitch's voice, I'm unable to speak. I hand the phone to Detective Connors and try to stifle my sobs.

"Mr. McElroy, this is Liam Connors. I'm here

with Mrs. McElroy—"

Mitch's voice cracks as he blurts, "Is she all right?"

Connors flinches and pulls the phone from his ear, "Yes, she's okay. Mr. McElroy, your wife had another visit from Psycho-man late yesterday—"

"WHAT?" Mitch again interrupts.

"Hold on, she was in the midst of telling me about it when you called. I'm going to put you on speaker so we can all participate in the conversation." Connors looks at me and I nod as I dab at my tears.

"Sam," Mitch says obviously straining to maintain his composure, "I should've been—"

"I'm okay," I say not allowing him to finish his sentence. "Attila rescued me." Reigning in my emotions, I relate the encounter as best I can. Neither Mitch nor Connors interrupt my narration. When I finish, I hear Mitch sigh. "Thank God the cops kept the red paint smear out of the news," he mummers.

"Sometimes we get it right," Connors comments. "Since the hurricane crisis is over, I'm going to reassign an officer to your wife and insist that she not venture out without police protection and when she's home someone be here with her. In your absence, rest assured we'll keep careful watch on your home."

"I didn't mean any disrespect..." Mitch replies.

"None taken," Connors says.

Having regained my composure somewhat, I divert the direction of the conversation away from me in an effort to dissipate Mitch's concern. I realize that was a lot to lay on him and after a moment I detect a sigh of relief on Mitch's end of the line, so I ask, "How'd your mission go?"

"It was a success. The flight was a bit bumpy, but we arrived in Orlando in one piece. I called ahead and an ambulance was waiting on the tarmac. Cindy was admitted to St. Luke's Children's' Hospital and diagnosed with a concussion just as you suspected. She's going to be all right, Sam, thanks to your quick thinking. It's doubtful she has brain damage."

"Another miracle," I say. "When are you coming home?"

"I'm at the airport as we speak and as soon as I get clearance, I'm headed home. Not going to wait for Cindy to be released from the hospital, no telling how long that will be. Air traffic has been restored and Renee and Cindy can fly home commercial. I need to be with you right now—for your sake and mine."

Feeling relived, I say, "Attila will be glad to have you back home."

After a pause, Mitch asks, "Anyone else?"

"Who did you have in mind?"

"Someone my life would not be the same without."

"Then why the delay?" I ask.

"I'll be there even if I have to ditch the plane and parachute in."

• • •

As soon as Connors leaves, I batten down the hatches and lock the doors. I pull out an old Bible given to me by my grandfather and turn to Psalm 23:

The Lord is my shepherd; I shall not want.
*   In verdant pastures he gives me repose;*
Beside restful waters he leads me;
*   he refreshes my soul.*
He guides me in right paths
*   for his name's sake.*
Even though I walk in the dark valley,
*   I fear no evil; for you are at my side*
With your rod and your staff
*   That give me courage.*

You spread the table before me
*   in the sight of my foes;*
You anoint my head with oil;
*   my cup overflows.*

*Only goodness and kindness follow
me all the days of my life;
And I shall dwell in the house of the
Lord for years to come.*

Chapter Nine

Cinco

Upon arriving home after his second encounter with Attila, Juan is frustrated beyond belief. He rants and raves as he paces around his apartment reliving the events of the evening. Because the sound of the storm drowns out his shouting and cursing there's little concern his neighbors will take notice.

Had her within my grasp! Juan puts his hands out in front of him poised in a choking motion and violently shakes them in the air. *Right here! Right here!* Looking at his outstretched hands, he again notices the fresh bite marks on his fists and the old ones on his arms and his ranting turns into rage. He throws wooden kitchen chairs against the wall, knocks over a table lamp, and swipes dishes from the kitchen counter scattering broken pieces helter-skelter across the floor.

After a few minutes of uncontrolled fury, Juan collapses on the sofa, emotionally and physically spent. He falls into a deep, restless sleep. When he awakens, the events of the night before come floating back. He clicks on the television set anxious for new coverage of his exploits and an update on the hurricane, The face of the female news anchor that fills the screen reminds him of Carmen. Juan sits up and watches with renewed interest.

At the conclusion of the newscast, the anchor signs off: "This is Maria Concha for WIRE. Stay tuned to Channel Seventeen for the latest news happening worldwide. I'm back in the newsroom tomorrow at seven a.m."

Juan's attention is piqued as he zeros in on another victim. He thereupon assigns Maria Concha the name *Cinco. Cuatro can wait.* Juan is immediately regenerated with having identified the next Jezebel marked for extermination. His previous MO, that is stalking his target, worked so well in the past, he decides not to deviate from the tried and true. *She's back at 7:00 a.m. tomorrow...* Juan looks up the address of WIRE in the phonebook.

Early the next morning Juan parks in a spot where he can watch the entrance to the television station. At precisely 8:15 a.m. *Cinco* exits the building. The winds in the aftermath of the hurricane blow her long dark hair around her face obscuring her features. However, Juan instinctively knows this is his target. He watches her cross to the employee's parking lot, and as she drives past his vehicle, he follows her.

Instead of going straight home, Maria turns

into the parking lot of Dave's Diner, and maneuvers her Camaro into the last parking spot. Juan is forced to drive around the block searching for a place to park. Much to his chagrin, traffic is slow because of the debris littering the streets. Police patrols on duty at the major thoroughfares motion for drivers to take turns going around large objects still blocking the roadway. By the time Juan gets back to the diner, Maria's car is gone. *She must have ordered take out.* Her actions convey that she has a familiarity with Dave's Diner, so Juan concludes this is a daily routine.

• • •

At 8:30 the next morning, Juan drives to the diner and takes a table by a window where he can watch the parking lot. He orders a bagel and coffee, something quick so he can leave on a moment's notice without attracting attention. When he sees Maria's vehicle approach, he goes to the cashier. By the time Maria picks up her takeout order and exits the diner, Juan's in his car waiting.

From a safe distance, Juan follows Maria home. Now armed with her work schedule, her address, and her morning routine, he begins to formulate a plan. He reasons that since he charmed the lovely Carmen into dating him, there's a chance that Maria might also be lured into going out with him and then...

In order to set his trap, Juan spruces up his appearance and makes it a point to show up at Dave's Diner on a daily basis. He always takes the same table close to the cashier and arranges to be in the checkout line either in front of or behind Maria. Being a television personality, Maria is used to people ogling her, so she isn't surprised when Juan engages her in conversation.

"Hey, aren't you Maria Concha?" Juan asks as they stand in line waiting to pay.

Maria turns and flashes Juan a broad smile, "Yes, I am."

"I thought so," Juan comments. "I watch WIRE every morning as I get ready for work."

"Thanks, you're obviously a gentleman of distinction," Maria says, and they both laugh.

Juan snatches Maria's check from her fingers, "Here, let me get this. You do such a great public service with your reporting, it's the least I can do."

"Why…why, thank you," Maria says and smiles. "Not just for buying my breakfast but for the compliment. It's important to have feedback from our viewers. We strive for excellence."

"And it appears you're accomplishing your goal," Juan replies as he places both checks, his and hers, on the counter along with a twenty-dollar bill.

Once outside the diner, Juan asks, "Where are you parked?"

Maria points and says, "Right over there."

"I'll walk you to your car..."

"Ah, no need for that. Thank you anyway," Maria replies.

Having assumed a dapper-dan-style masquerade, Juan says, "As you wish, madam. Have a good day," and turns in the opposite direction. He can feel Maria's eyes on his back as he strolls toward his vehicle whistling a tune.

By the end of the week, Maria aborts the takeout orders and is now sharing a table with Juan at Dave's Diner. Wanting to appear to be a big spender, Juan buys Maria's breakfast each day.

"I can't allow you to pay all the time," Maria says and reaches across the table toward Juan's check.

Juan covers her hand with his, "Now, now, it's my pleasure. After all, you're the one who dubbed me a *gentleman of distinction*. You wouldn't want to take that away from me, now would you?"

Maria doesn't pull her hand away when Juan touches it. Sensing she's receptive to his overtures, he continues, "I see where *The Strand* is showcasing some old movies this month. I believe *Casa Blanca* is playing there now. Would you like to go some evening? We can have dinner before the movie."

"*Casa Blanca* is one of my all-time favorites! I'd love to go but only on the condition you agree we go Dutch."

Juan flinches. He doesn't know what *Dutch* means, but in order not to appear ignorant, he agrees. "Okay by me. When would you like to go?" he asks.

Maria looks thoughtful. "I'm up early every weekday but don't work weekends. How 'bout Friday so I can sleep in on Saturday?"

"Friday it is! And dinner?" Juan asks.

"There's a nice seafood restaurant on the pier, it's called *Nautilus*. I can meet you there around six and after dinner we can catch the movie."

Juan stiffens when Maria says *Nautilus*, but quickly recovers. The last night he spent with Carmen flashes through his mind. "Yes, I'm familiar with the *Nautilus*," he says. He also notices Maria, like Carmen, wants to meet rather than have him pick her up. *Jezebels! They're all alike! Probably has a live-in.*

• • •

When Juan arrives at work the next day, he stops by Rusty's office and taps on the open door. Rusty looks up from his paperwork, smiles and beckons Juan in.

"Juan, what can I do for you?" Rusty asks.

"I have a dumb question. Since I'm not familiar with American slang even though I studied English," Juan says, as he steps inside the office, "can you tell me what to *go Dutch* means?"

"Sure, take a seat," Rusty says and points to a chair. He turns and takes the Pyrex coffee pot from a hotplate on his credenza and raises his brow Juan's direction. Juan nods.

As Rusty pours a cup for Juan and tops off his own cup, he replies, "To *go Dutch* means that each individual pays his or her own way."

"Oh," Juan says. "Guess I should've remembered that."

"Hey, man!" Rusty exclaims, "You're a lucky guy if you got a gal who wants to *go Dutch*."

• • •

Juan arrives at the *Nautilus* on Friday a little before six and requests a booth in the back away from other customers. When he sees Maria enter, he leans out of the booth and waves to her. She joins him.

"Good evening," he says.

Maria looks around their dim, isolated surroundings. "This is quaint," she says, apparently noticing there are several unoccupied tables toward the front close to windows with views of the ocean and not so secluded.

"Would you prefer we sit elsewhere?" Juan asks.

Maria, apparently embarrassed that Juan picked up on her obvious displeasure, replies, "Oh, no. This is fine," and slides onto the seat across from him.

A waiter appears with two glasses of ice water and hands them each a menu. When he returns to take their order, Maria requests separate checks.

"Nonsense," Juan argues. "Put this on one check," he says looking up at the waiter.

"Oh, no," Maria counters. "Remember, we agreed to *go Dutch*."

Juan, not wanting to cause a scene and attract unwanted attention, nods his consent. He resents Maria for making him look cheap in front of the waiter. Suddenly, what he anticipated was going to be a pleasant dinner turns awkward. Maria must feel the tension as well. Dinner conversation is sparse, and Juan's eager to have it over with.

The waiter brings their checks, and after they each pay, Maria says, "Would you mind if we skip the movie? I…I have a headache."

"I'm sorry. Of course, if you don't feel well…" Juan pauses, and not wanting to let the opportunity slip by, he adds, "Perhaps a stroll on the pier would clear your head."

The sun is setting, and a chilly breeze is coming off the water. "Humm, I don't know…" Maria says. The anxiety in her voice is evident as she glances around the almost deserted pier.

"Ah, come on. It'll be fun," Juan encourages.

"Well, all right," Maria replies, apparently feeling guilty about having spoiled their evening.

Juan guides Maria to the exact spot where, only a few months ago, he and Carmen sat on wooden bench just before he killed her.

"Back home in Cuba," Juan says, "I liked to go diving. I'd take my scuba gear and spend hours in the ocean exploring aquatic life. It's fascinating. Do you dive?"

"Oh, heavens no!" Maria blurts. "I can barely swim in backyard pools much less the ocean."

That was all the information Juan needed to proceed with his diabolical scheme. He scoots closer to Maria, and pretending to put his arm around her shoulders in a romantic gesture, he grips her by the neck with one hand, and with his other hand applies pressure to her carotid artery halting the normal flow of blood to her brain. She doesn't put up much of a struggle and a minute later she's unconscious. When she slumps against him, Juan takes quick inventory of the surroundings. No one is near. He quickly removes a silver Sigma Delta sorority charm bracelet from her wrist and then shoves her into the ocean. Slipping the bracelet into his pocket, Juan stands at the edge of the pier and watches as she disappears beneath the surface of the water. Juan strolls casually back to his car, secure that no one has noticed him. He feels satisfied with having rid the world of another Jezebel.

• • •

After hanging the Sigma Delta charm bracelet on the wall next to his other trophies, Juan pulls the covers up tightly around him and dreams of the next victim. It's a deep uninterrupted sleep—one that causes him to smile in his slumber.

Chapter Ten

Reunited

I'm at the window watching for Mitch, and as soon as I see his car turn into the driveway, I rush out to meet him. Attila outruns me and when Mitch steps from the car, he's swamped as Attila and I vie for his attention.

Rubbing Attila's head, Mitch says, "Hey, buddy, I missed you too." Mitch then gathers me into an embrace and whispers in my ear, "But I missed you more."

I whisper back, "Don't let you-know-who hear you say that. He might turn tail the next time Psycho-man shows up and let Psycho-man get rid of his competition."

"Won't matter. I plan to be here if there is a next time. I can't even describe the feeling I had when I learned you were once again in danger." Mitch looks thoughtful as he rubs the back of his neck, "I'm going to stick to you like glue until this maniac is captured."

• • •

Two days after Mitch arrives home, the headlines of the *Key West Communiqué* tell the story:

The body of Maria Concha was discovered yesterday evening on a deserted stretch of beach just a mile from the spot where the body of Carmen Ochoa was found four months ago. Concha, a popular television personality, was an anchor on the weekday morning newscast, WIRE.

Authorities aren't commenting, pending the results of an autopsy, but it appears to this reporter that Concha is number four on the killer's ever-growing list of victims. A photo of Concha appears on page two of this edition of the Communiqué alongside the other three victims. They bear an uncanny resemblance to one another.

Your help is needed. If you have any information, even if you think it's insignificant, please contact the KWPD or MCSO. And we remind our female readers to constantly be aware of their surroundings and travel in pairs for their own safety. With a killer on the loose, no one is safe.

Mitch and I just stare at each other after we read the article. No words are necessary. The killer's determination cannot be underestimated.

. . .

Jimmy Haskell, a member of the wait staff, arrives at the *Nautilus* a few minutes before his afternoon shift begins. *The Key West Communiqué* is spread on the counter in the kitchen and Jimmy reads the article as he ties his apron around his waist. Curious to see the photos of the killer's victims, he flips to page two. He instantly recognizes the photo of Maria Concha and immediately calls 911. Upon identifying the caller and the nature of the call, the 911 operator transfers Jimmy to the detective division.

"Detective Connors, how can I help you?" Connors asks. The detective division has been swamped with so many false reports, they're now at the point of just going through the motions.

"My name is Jimmy Haskell. I'm a waiter at the *Nautilus*. When I saw the pictures of the victims in the newspaper, I remembered that a few days ago I served Maria Concha and her dinner companion. I don't recall if it was on the date of her drowning or not."

Connors jumps to his feet. "Where are you now?" he asks.

"I'm at work."

"Stay there. We're on our way."

Connors picks up Lewis as he rushes from

the building and they waste no time getting to the *Nautilus*. Jimmy is waiting on a table when he sees them come in. Even though they're not in uniform, he instinctively knows they're the fuzz. He watches as the cashier points him out to the detectives, and as they move toward him, he asks a coworker to cover his station for a few minutes.

"Afternoon, officers," he says. "There's an empty office off the kitchen we can use. If you'll follow me…"

Once behind closed doors, Connors begins the interview. "You say you waited on Concha and her dinner companion?"

"Yes, Sir," Jimmy replies.

"Tell us what happened," Connors says. Lewis doesn't look up. He's poised to take notes.

"Sure," Jimmy says. "The guy came in first, and even though we weren't very busy, he insisted on a booth in the back. I thought that was odd because the front tables have excellent views of the Gulf and not all were occupied. In fact, customers often waive their place in line to wait for a table closer to the front just to enjoy the view. I overheard the dude tell Beverly, the hostess, that he was waiting for someone."

"Okay, then what?" Connors asks.

"Well, I noticed the guy kept a close eye on the

entrance and as soon as the bombshell comes in, he stands and waves to her."

"Okay, go on," Connors says sounding somewhat irritated at having to keep prompting Jimmy.

"The chick was pretty special and in my opinion the dude was way out of his league. When she approached, she didn't look too excited about the location of the booth. I was on my way to their table with water and overheard her say 'This is quaint,' or something like that in a sarcastic tone. I noticed the guy looked sheepish and muttered something I couldn't hear, after which the chick slid onto the seat across from him." Jimmy pauses and a thoughtful expression crosses his face. "Is the Crime Stoppers' reward for the serial killer still in effect?" he asks.

Connors appears to be exasperated. He answers in a curt voice, "Yes. Information leading to the arrest and conviction of a criminal entitles the whistleblower to compensation. Now, continue with your story."

Jimmy nods. If he detected Connors' irritation, it didn't show. "When I took their order, the chick asked me to put their meals on separate checks."

Lewis looks up and Connors raises his brow, "Separate checks?"

"Yeah. When the guy insisted on one check, the chick argued with him saying something about them having agreed to go Dutch. The guy looked embarrassed."

"That's really weird. What else?" Connors asks, in a more conciliatory tone.

"Well, nothing out of the ordinary. When I took them their checks, the guy seemed anxious to leave and stood up before I left the table. One thing that seemed odd to me was that the dude was dressed pretty nice but when he stood, I noticed he had on a pair of beat up sneakers and the left one had a red paint smear on it."

"Bingo!" Connors blurts. His exuberance is evident as he asks, "Did he pay with a card or cash?"

"Cash, and he left a nice tip," Jimmy says with a smile.

It was apparent Connors was pumped up. "Can you remember anything else?" he asks.

"Nope," then after a pause, Jimmy adds, "Well, maybe. I come to work before the doors open to get my station set up and help with bringing in the cooking supplies. The last couple of days, I've noticed a car parked in the same spot in the parking lot. Seems odd that someone who didn't work here would leave their car in the lot for that long—"

"Show us the car," Lewis interrupts and both he and Connors stand.

• • •

Jimmy leads the detectives across the parking lot to where the abandoned car is parked. As they approach the vehicle, Lewis calls in the license plates. Moments later he's informed the vehicle is registered to Maria Concha. He relates the information to Connors and Connors blurts, "Get a crime scene unit over here ASAP." Taking Jimmy aside, Connors says, "Thanks, kid, you've been very helpful. You can get back to work now. If any arrests come from your information, we'll make sure to alert Crime Stoppers and see that you are properly rewarded."

Jimmy nods and heads back to the restaurant. When Jimmy's out of earshot, Connors glances at Lewis, and asks a rhetorical question, "Her date had a smear of red paint on his left tennis shoe. Sound familiar?"

"Paydirt!" Lewis exclaims as the two focus their attention on the baby blue Camaro.

Connors and Lewis each pull a pair of latex gloves from their pockets. Trying the door handle on the driver's side, they discover the doors are unlocked, Connors remarks, "Let's see if the car has anything to offer." Lewis moves to the passenger side.

In order not to disturb any physical evidence, such as hair or fibers, the detectives don't enter the vehicle, they examine it by peering through the open doors. As soon as he opens the passenger door, Lewis discovers a day planner on the seat. He carefully opens it and thumbs to the date Jimmy said he served Concha and her date. Penciled in at the 6:00 p.m. slot were the initials JS and the word *Nautilus*.

"Hey, Liam, think I've found something," he says, and glances at Connors.

Connors immediately rounds the car and joins Lewis. Without removing the day planner from the car seat, Connors examines the entry. "Looks like our killer's initials are JS," he muses as he straightens up. "Feels like we've just won the lottery. First the red paint connection and now this."

• • •

Maria's Camaro was impounded and examined by forensics. Hair, fibers, and incidental debris were collected, marked, and packaged in plastic bags by the crime scene investigators. All evidence was later examined with a fine-toothed comb, but at the end of the day, nothing of any significance, other than the notation in Maria's day planner was discovered. The remainder of the evidence pointed back to Maria. It appeared no one else had been in her car. Her home was also searched. There was nothing out of the ordinary to even hint as to who JS was. Even her coworkers were unable to put a name to the initials. It was determined that Maria lived alone and was extremely private about her personal life. An attempt to identify the mystery man for the time being reached a dead end.

• • •

Connors sat at his desk. He appeared to be very frustrated that, even with the new evidence, the investigation had come to somewhat of a standstill. Evans, a seasoned reporter, usually listened to his instincts. He had phoned earlier and asked to see Connors. When he enters Connor's office, he remarks, "Hey, Liam, you look like you just lost your last friend."

"That bad, huh?" Connors mummers.

"Anything I can do to ease the pain?" Evans asks.

"Maybe," Connors replies. "You've been pretty insightful in the past and I respect your input. Often fresh eyes can spot the elephant in the room everyone else is missing. If I let you in on the latest, you promise to keep it under wraps unless I okay its release?"

"Hell, yes, man! I haven't betrayed your trust

in the past and don't intend to now," says Evans.

Connors nods and passes a folder to Evans. He remains silent as Evans reads the report. When Evans finishes, he looks up at Connors. "We knew about the red paint on his shoe and kept that out of the news. That could be very important when it comes to identifying him. Now, having his initials is another breakthrough."

Evans taps his pencil against a notepad. "I'm thinking with these two pieces of information, if we run the story, someone may be able to connect the dots. How many men out there have red paint on their left shoe and have the initials JS?" Evans looks at Connors, "What do you think?"

"I've been kicking that around. If we run the story, JS goes underground and destroys the evidence. And if we don't at least try, he'll keep killing with impunity…" Connors replies. "Seems like we're between a rock and a hard spot…"

"If we get lucky, someone may know who he is by putting the paint and initials together and perhaps an arrest can be made before he can escape…" Evans bites the end of his pencil and peers at Connors.

"Highly unlikely," says Connors. "This maniac thrives on being the headlines and is probably the first one to read the newspaper every day. As soon as he sees the story, he'll boogie. And who's to say he won't relocate to some other city and finish off the top ten, including a return engagement with McElroy. He's made two failed attempts on her life already. With four dead, that leaves six innocent women at his mercy."

As the two men sit in reflective silence, Connors' phone rings. "Detective Connors speaking," he answers.

"Ah, yes, detective. I'm…I'm…I'm the cashier at Dave's Diner on Aruba and First," the caller says.

"Okay. Who am I speaking to?"

"Delores Watson."

"What can I do for you, Ms. Watson?" Connors asks and furrows his brow.

"I know Maria Concha," Delores answers.

Connors sits up straighter. "How do you know her?" he asks.

"Well, not personally but I know who she is. She comes, or I should say came, into the diner almost every workday morning and ordered takeout."

"Okay, go on."

"About a month ago a stranger started coming in about the same time as Ms. Concha. I noticed him paying close attention to her. He'd manage to get into the checkout line either in front of or behind her. It wasn't long before they got friendly and he started paying her checks and they'd leave together."

"Can you describe the stranger?" Connors asks and glances toward Evans who only hears Connors' end of the conversation.

"Yes. I took his money every day for over a month. I was suspicious of him from the get-go because of the way he stalked Ms. Concha."

"What does he look like?" Connors persists. His tone of voice reflects his patience is growing thin.

"Well, he has a slight accent, I think Cuban. He has dark hair and eyes, about six-foot-tall and I'd say in the neighborhood of one-hundred eighty pounds, quite muscular."

"Would you be able to recognize him if you saw him again or maybe a photograph of him?"

"Not sure," Dolores says.

Connors' wide grin conveyed a positive message to Evans. "Did you see what he was driving and perhaps his license plate number?"

"No. My cashier position is not in line with the parking lot, so no, I didn't."

"Humm, anything else you can remember about him?" Connors asks.

"I remember that on most days he wore a T-shirt that advertised a fish distributorship. I think it was Donavon's or something like that. All

I know is that it was not the name of any of the distributors we use."

"Ms. Watson. It's important that you come to the station and make a formal statement. In the meantime, I'd ask that you not share this information with anyone."

"Of course. Will tomorrow morning be soon enough?" Delores asks.

"Indeed. If I'm not here, Detective Lewis can take your statement. And thank you for coming forward."

"You're welcome. I wasn't sure this would be of any help but felt it was my civic duty," Delores says.

"Any leads we get are important. Thank you once again," Connors says and hangs up the phone. Then to Evans he says, "We got a description and possible place of employment." The papers on Connors' desk scatter as he roughly jerks open his phonebook. He turns to *Fish Distributors*. There is no Donovan's but there is a Dougan's. After jotting down an address, Connors jumps up, grabs his jacket from the back of his chair, and heads for the door. Once in the corridor, he shouts, "Lewis, front and center!"

Racing from the police station, Connors and Lewis take the steps two at a time. When they reach their cruiser, Connors jumps into the driver's seat.

He's in such a frenzy, and apparently ignoring the oncoming traffic, he guns out barely avoiding a collision.

"Take it easy, man," Lewis cautions, looking back over his shoulder. "What's up anyway?"

On the way to Dugan's Fish Distributors, Connors fills Lewis in on the phone call from Delores Watson. "This could be our lucky day," Connors says.

"Provided we survive," Lewis replies, hanging onto the handle above the passenger door.

Connors ignores the sarcastic remark obviously referring to his driving. There is no time to squander.

Evans was left sitting in Connors' office. Perplexed, he sensed something significant was afoot and rushes from Connors' office. The vehicle Evans is driving is parked at the curb and he makes it just in time to see Connors screech from the parking lot. Evans slams his car into gear and follows the detectives. Fortunately, this day he's driving his wife's SUV and figures he won't be recognized by Connors and Lewis. It's not in his nature to be devious. However, he's not about to allow the opportunity of a scoop to be squandered. Besides, his aim is the same as the police: to catch a serial killer.

Chapter Eleven

Two Plus Two = Four

Rusty Dougan is sitting behind his desk when the detectives are ushered into his office.

"Afternoon, gentlemen," Rusty says as he stands and extends a hand. "Come in and grab a seat."

After shaking hands and introducing themselves, Connors and Lewis sit down.

"How can I help the KWPD?" Rusty asks and rears back, crossing his legs looking very casual.

Connors is chomping at the bit and gets right to it. "We're tracking down a person of interest and we have information that he may be working for you."

"Really? Person of interest…What's his name?" Rusty asks.

"We don't know. We're hoping you could provide that."

"Okay. Do you have a description?"

Lewis takes over, "He's of Cuban descent, about six foot, one-hundred and eighty pounds."

Rusty laughs. "That describes about half of my employees."

"We also know his initials are JS."

"Okay, that narrows it down somewhat," Rusty

says and as he turns, engages his computer. Bringing up a list of employees, he scrolls down to the letter S. "Let's see," he says, "we have a Jose Sanchez, Joseph Santana and Juan Santiago."

Connors says, "Mr. Dougan, the individual we're looking for has been identified by a couple of witnesses as having a smear of red paint on his left shoe. Do any one of those three fit that description?"

"Humm, yep. I think I remember Juan having dropped a paint brush loaded with red paint when he helped repaint the trim on the shop about six months ago. He was very vocal about having ruined his new tennis shoes."

Connors looks at Lewis. Neither say anything.

Rusty continues, "I hope he's not in serious trouble. He's been with me for over two years now and a damn good worker. In fact, he's pretty naïve when it comes to American customs despite being well-versed in the English language which he attributes to an aunt who was educated in the United States."

"What do you mean?" Lewis asks.

"Why, just the other day, he came into my office, and sounding somewhat embarrassed, asked me what it meant to go Dutch."

Without hesitation, Connors asks, "Do you know where Juan is right now?"

"Should be on the loading dock," Rusty replies. "I can have someone go get him."

"No! I mean, no need for that. If you just point the way, we can find him," Connors says.

• • •

Juan had been helping unload the catch. It's a hot day, and after taking a crate inside the building and placing it in the cooler, he heads for the water fountain which is just beyond Rusty's office. The office door is slightly ajar, and Juan can hear part of the conversation between Rusty and the detectives. Fear grips him as he realizes the conversation is about him. He carefully backs away from the office, and much to the surprise of his fellow workers, bolts from the building and races to the parking lot.

• • •

When the three men gathered in Rusty's office and hear a commotion in the parking lot they rush to the window. They watch a vehicle spew gravel as it speeds toward the street. Before it exits the parking lot, another vehicle races toward it from the right. The second vehicle rams into the passenger side door of the first vehicle. The hood on the first vehicle pops up and steam streams from the engine and the vehicle stalls. To add to the chaos, the impact triggered the car alarms on both vehicles creating an earsplitting noise.

The driver of the first car seems to be unhurt. He flings the car door open and flees on foot. However, the driver of the second car remains slumped over the steering wheel without moving.

Connors glances at Rusty and barks, "Do you have an address for Santiago?"

Rusty rushes back to his computer, and a moment later says, "He lives in the Coral Apartments, seven twenty-six Gulf Way, Number B seventeen."

Rushing to the office door, Connors shouts to Lewis, "Call it in! Put out an APB on Santiago, get a team to cover his apartment and a tow truck to confiscate his car. But first, get an ambulance over here ASAP. I fear the driver of the second car might be seriously injured."

Connors then races from Rusty's office across the parking lot to where the damaged cars are stalled. Getting closer to the scene, Connors recognizes that the driver of the second vehicle is Evans. He forces the driver's door open and assesses the damage. A deflated air bag drapes over the steering wheel and blood runs down Evans' face from a gash on his head. Upon closer inspection, Connors observes Evans' left arm is hanging at an odd angle and concludes that it's broken. Connors immediately applies pressure to the head wound and slows the bleeding. Within minutes he hears a siren as an ambulance approaches. He stands and frantically waves at the ambulance. As soon as it arrives, Connors steps back to give the EMTs space to work. Much to his relief, he hears Evans groan.

"Is he going to be all right?" Connors asks the EMT working on Evans' head wound.

"I think so. Head wounds bleed profusely." Still working on Evans, the tech continues, "The brain requires an enormous amount of oxygen to do its job. Consequently, a person's heart pumps about twenty percent of the blood to the brain."

Before Connors can reply, Lewis pulls up beside him having retrieved their cruiser from the employee parking lot. The EMT is now thoroughly engrossed in treating Evans. After taking one last look at the scene, Connors jumps in beside Lewis.

Lewis points to Connors' seatbelt in an unspoken gesture for Connors to fasten it. "How's Evans?" he asks without taking his eye off oncoming traffic.

Complying with Lewis' request, Connors fastens his seatbelt, and replies, "EMTs are on the job…I think he's going to make it. If Evans hadn't intervened, we'd have lost Santiago for sure. Santiago had a pretty good head start. Then again, for Evans to have followed on his own was not such a good idea."

"Right. However, as it is, it's still iffy the APB will produce anything," Lewis says.

"But having our suspect afoot is much better than in a vehicle," Connors replies. "He can't be very far ahead of us."

•••

Juan, although shaken by the impact is not seriously injured. Able to jump from his damaged car, he immediately heads for his apartment. Fortunately for him, it's only about a mile, as the crow flies, from the fish distributorship and he takes shortcuts through neighborhoods and vacant lots. Having overheard the conversation about the red paint on his tennis shoe, he approaches a neighborhood dumpster. There he removes the shoes and tosses them into the dumpster.

•••

Colonel Samuel Culpepper, as he calls himself, is a vagrant and a regular around the Sandy Hills subdivision. The neighborhood knows him as Sammy. Today, as Sammy is making his rounds, he watches Juan toss something into a dumpster and then rush off. Curious as to what was thrown into the trash in such a hurry, Sammy shuffles over to the dumpster. Since the trash hadn't yet been collected, the shoes are on top of the piles of plastic bags and easy to retrieve.

Sammy spots the shoes right away. "Would ja just look at that," he mumbles. Sammy has a habit of talking to himself or some imaginary companion, no one knows for sure which. "That fella done went and throwd away some perfectly fine shoes. Unh, unh!"

· · ·

Sammy pulled the discarded shoes from the dumpster under the watchful eye of Bethany Oglesby, a spinster who lives across the street from the dumpster pickup site. Being a busy body, Bethany was inclined to keep tabs on what was happening around the neighborhood. At the time, Juan sped past, Bethany was out pruning her rose bushes. She paused in her work to watch the stranger come pounding down the street, stop long enough to remove his shoes, and toss them into the trash, then keep on running in his bare feet. *How odd*, she thought. *But at least he tossed them into the receptacle and not onto the street or tie the laces together and toss them over the electric wires.*

A few minutes later, Bethany, still looking in the direction of the dumpster, watched Sammy approach and reach in and pull the shoes from the trash. He plopped down by the dumpster and replaced his tattered shoes with Juan's. Bethany would later tell the detectives that Sammy seemed "pleased as punch with his good fortune and pranced around like a carnival pony." She said she overhead him say, as he paraded up and down in front of the dumpster, "'Tan't never had nuttin' this grand. Unh, unh!"

Bethany said her curiosity got the better of her, so she set aside her pruning and walked across the street to where Sammy was admiring his new shoes and asks, "You find some shoes?"

"Yes, ma'am, indeed I did. Ain't they just fine?" Sammy asked, looking down at his feet.

"Yes, Sammy, they are," Bethany said she replied. Bethany later stated that Sammy's smile "stretched from ear-to-ear."

. . .

Running the rest of the way home barefooted, Juan arrives before the police show up. He slams into his apartment and hastily jerks his souvenirs and newspaper clippings from the wall. Jamming them into his pants pockets, he grabs a pair of worn leather shoes from his closet, and slipping into them, exits out the backway.

Once outside, Juan cautiously circles to the front of the apartment building. He stops and ducks back behind the corner of the building when he notices a uniformed officer standing at the entrance.

When the officer turns his back, Juan worms his way to a clump of shrubs a few yards from where he's hiding. Everything happens so fast, and with nowhere to go and no one to turn to, Juan finds himself in a confused state of mind. He hastily takes inventory of his situation and determines he has less than $10.00 in his pockets. He regrets not taking time to get the meager savings he has stashed in an envelope taped to the underside of a dresser drawer. *Money's the least of my worries. I can always steal what I need.*

Terrified he would be caught with the incriminating evidence on his person, Juan decides he has no choice but to get rid of his precious souvenirs. He can't afford to be discovered while they're still in his possession. His options are limited, and as he looks around for a hiding spot, Juan discovers the soil is soft and sandy and decides to bury the evidence. He digs a hole with his hands in the clump of shrubs and stuffs the souvenirs and newspaper clippings into the hole and covers them with sand. Juan is so engrossed in his predicament, he doesn't notice a dog sniffing around on the other side of the shrubs.

• • •

Confident he's outsmarted the law, Juan devises a plan on how to return to his apartment. He reasons that by acting innocent, he could pull it off. The only crime they can pin on him now is leaving the scene of an accident. He can explain his running away was because his green card had expired, and he ran to avoid deportation.

Juan waits for the officer to turn his back before he leaves his hiding place. When the officer turns, Juan scrambles to the walkway leading from the parking area to the apartment building. He hopes to appear as though he's coming from the parking lot. When Juan approaches the front of the apartment building, the officer stationed at the entrance stops him. The nameplate on the officer's uniform identifies him as M. Crowley. "Where you headed?" Crowley asks.

"Apartment B seventeen, I live here," Juan replies, trying to look casual.

Crowley looks Juan up and down. "You have some ID?" he asks.

Juan complies by extracting his driver's license from his wallet. Crowley studies the photo on the driver's license and then Juan's face. Juan can tell from the expression on the officer's face that the officer recognizes him as the person the authorities are looking for.

"Mr. Santiago," Crowley growls, "There's an APB out for your arrest."

"But…but, all I've done is leave the scene of an accident. I know it was wrong, but I was scared…" Juan stammers.

Just then Connors and Lewis pull up in front of the building. Apparently, seeing the officer engaging Juan, Connors jumps from the cruiser. "Afternoon, officer," he says to Crowley. "Who have we here?" he asks knowing full well who the detainee is.

"Hey, Liam," Crowley replies and hands Connors Juan's driver's license. "This man's name is Juan Santiago and says he lives here."

Connors examines the license. "Are you here illegally?"

"No, well maybe. My green card has expired…" Juan answers.

"Why did you leave the scene of an accident?" Lewis asks.

"Afraid I'd be deported!" Juan is now visibly unnerved.

"We have witnesses who claim you may be involved in a string of murders—" Connors begins. Juan's livid. "What! That's not true! You're bluffing," he shouts, and then composing himself asks more calmly, "What witnesses?"

Connors ignores Juan's question and instead asks, "If all you've done is leave the scene of an accident, as you contend, would you consent to having your home searched?"

Juan is trapped. If he says no, they'll suspect him of something and search anyway. If he says okay, they may find something. However, he's so confident he's removed all of the incriminating evidence, and in order to look like the innocent person he was attempting to portray, he agrees to the search. He replies with a weak, "Okay."

"Need for you to sign this consent form," Lewis says. "It'll take only a minute to fill out."

While Lewis completes the form consenting to the search, Connors summons a CSI team.

After Juan signs the form, Lewis asks for the key to Juan's apartment and Juan is placed in a police cruiser. The doors are closed, and the vehicle is parked facing away from the apartment complex. Juan is unable to see or hear what's going outside the confines of the backseat of the police cruiser. Although he's sure there's nothing to connect him to the murders, he's still anxious and strains his neck trying to peer out of the back window.

• • •

While the detectives wait outside the building for the CSI team to arrive, a child pushes through the apartment complex's double glass doors. Squeezing past them, the little girl stands on the pavement and shouts, "Here, Coco, come on girl!"

"Get that kid outta here," Lewis orders. Before Crawley can act upon the command, a curly honey-colored toy poodle emerges from the shrubs and runs to where the girl is kneeling.

"Coco, good dog," the girl says and pets the little ball of fur on the head.

Connors, watching the girl's interaction with the dog, steps closer. "What's your name?" he asks.

"Mary Alice, and this is Coco," the girl says still petting the dog.

"How old are you, Mary Alice?"

"Five," Mary Alice replies, and holds up a thumb and four fingers. She turns her attention to the dog, "Coco's three." Mary Alice then cocks her head, and looking at Coco's face, she says, "What's this," and pulls a small chain from the dog's mouth.

Connors is immediately interested in the find. "Can I see that, Mary Alice?" he asks.

Mary Alice places the item into Connors' outstretched hand. Connors examines it and realizes it's the custom-made silver bracelet with the Sigma Delta charm described to him by Maria Concha's sorority sisters. Connors looks up and glances around. He hadn't noticed from which direction the dog had come, so he asks Mary Alice. "Where was Coco hiding?"

Mary Alice points to the clump of shrubs, "Over there," she says. "That's a shady spot she likes. That's where she buries her bones."

Connors looks in the direction Mary Alice is pointing and then back at the apartment building. "What apartment do you live in?" he asks.

"C three. It's up there," Mary Alice says pointing toward the top of the façade.

Connors follows her gaze. "Thanks, sweetheart. You take Coco home now. I'll be by later to meet your parents."

"Oh, goodie. Then can I have the bracelet back?" she asks and gently picks up the dog.

"Maybe you'll get a different one," Connors replies, "one that'll fit your wrist better."

As soon as Mary Alice and Coco are back inside the apartment building, Connors summons Lewis. He holds his open hand out displaying the bracelet.

"No way!" Lewis exclaims as he recognizes the importance of the find. "How'd—"

"Apparently, the pooch was trying to hide or retrieve a bone and came up with the bracelet." Connors points to the clump of shrubs, "I'm thinking there could be more stuff buried in there."

Lewis nods. "Think we need a warrant to search the bushes?"

"Let's not chance it. I'll stay on site," Connors replies. "If these shrubs contain what I think they do…"

"Be back as soon as possible," Lewis says. "I think I can get a magistrate to issue a search warrant."

Moments later, the CSI unit arrives. Connors greets the lead investigator, Dave Jordan, known as D.J. among his peers. "Hey, D.J."

D.J. acknowledges Connors' greeting and asks, "What do we have here?"

Connors nods toward the cruiser, "Most likely our serial killer," he says.

D.J. frowns and says, "You must be joking!"

"No, wouldn't joke about that," Connors replies and fills D.J. in on the circumstances leading him and his team up to having been summoned. "We have a consent form signed by Santiago to search his residence. However, we're erring on the side of caution and Lewis just left to get a warrant to search the grounds."

"Good thinking," D.J. remarks. "We've lost cases before when over-zealous officers ignore the Fourth Amendment search warrant requirements." D.J. rubs the back of his neck. "I agree with you. This is far too important to take a chance on having the evidence, if any there be, thrown out on a technicality. Since you have the consent to search the residence, we'll start there," D.J. says and beckons to his team to follow him.

···

An hour later Lewis is back with a warrant to search the grounds. Connors and Lewis go to Juan's apartment where they find D.J. filling out some paperwork. He looks up as they enter and points to the wall above a weather-beaten desk.

"Appears there were several objects taped to that wall," D.J. says. "You can see a faint outline of some of them. Maybe newspaper clippings. You know how serials like to keep their press." Then pointing with his pen, D.J. says, "There's an old Underwood over there."

Both detectives immediately converge on the typewriter. Without touching it, Connors asks Lewis, "Can you tell if the e is worn?" Neither can control their excitement.

Lewis leans forward toward the area housing the keys and intently examines them. "Not without doing some typing, but I'm willing to bet a month's pay that it is," he replies.

"D.J., the typewriter could be the nail in Psycho-man's coffin. Would you process it ASAP?" Connors asks.

"Will do," D.J. snaps. It was evident from his

tone of voice that Connors had insulted him.

Realizing his *faux pas*, Connors jams his hands into his pants pockets. "Sorry, D.J. Didn't mean to tell you how to do your job. I'm not doing so hot, myself."

"That's okay, Amigo. We're all under pressure," D.J. replies. "Moses and Tolson are on their way down to search the bushes while I finish up here."

• • •

Connors and Lewis wait at the edge of the shrubs. Approximately, a half-hour later, Moses and Tolson crawl out of the underbrush.

"Did you find anything?" Connors asks in an anxious voice.

Moses is carrying several plastic evidence bags that are marked, initialed, and sealed with red tape. He holds them up for Connors to see. Because of the chain of custody requirement, Moses must keep the evidence in his possession. However, even though Connors cannot touch it, he's allowed to look at the evidence through the transparent plastic bags. At this point he doesn't know the significance of the diamond ring, hair clip or gold cross necklace, but because the Sigma Delta bracelet apparently belonged to the fourth victim, he's almost certain the other three items belonged to the first three victims. The newspaper articles are wrinkled and torn. They're placed in separate plastic bags.

"Looks like we've caught us a serial killer!" he says.

As the four men walk back to where the police vehicles are parked, Moses comments, "Don't think we can get any decent prints from the items."

"Why not!" Connors blurts.

"Well, the sand under the brush is still damp from all the rain Dorinda dumped. Coupled with being damp, especially the news articles, with the dog scratching at the items, it's pretty iffy there would be any identifiable prints left. In fact, some of the newspaper articles are almost unrecognizable."

Lewis looks over at Connors and it appears to him that Connors is on the verge of a meltdown. Without fingerprints, there's virtually nothing to connect Juan to the items retrieved from the bushes except the close proximity to his residence which in and of itself is no insignificant thing.

• • •

Back at headquarters, Connors and Lewis are sitting in Connors' office when they get the call from D.J. "They match," D.J. says. "The letter e is the final nail in the coffin. It's pretty worn and is a perfect match to the letter e on the notes."

Connors gives Lewis the high-sign, and as soon as he ends the call, says, "Come on, Jim, let's go interrupt the DA's afternoon coffee break."

With their police reports in hand, Connors and Lewis are ushered into Turnbow's office.

"Been waiting for you," Turnbow says. He removes his jacket and loosens his tie before sitting down behind his desk. "Received a call from the PD saying you were on your way." Still in his first term as DA, Turnbow is eager to prove his worth. Prosecuting and convicting a serial killer would certainly enhance his chances of being elected Attorney General someday.

Turnbow accepts the paperwork Connors hands him. He frowns as he studies the reports. After reading them, he sits back in his chair and just shakes his head. "Juan Santiago certainly has a lot of explaining to do. The question is whether there's enough circumstantial evidence to get a conviction. Remember Juan doesn't have to prove his innocence or anything for that matter. It's up to us to prove his guilt beyond a reasonable doubt. That's an immense burden unlike in a civil case where it's proof by a greater weight of the evidence.

"The question is whether red paint on his tennis shoe, having a typewriter with one of the letters matching a distinctive mark on notes sent to the newspaper and you two finding incriminating items on the fringe of his apartment building complex are enough."

"Shouldn't the typewriter connection in itself be enough to at least get past a preliminary hearing?" Connors asks anxiously.

"So, you get past a preliminary hearing," Turnbow says, "then what? You still have a trial to contend with. Just because our suspect typed the notes doesn't necessarily mean he's the killer. Someone else may very well have committed the murders and the typist is merely trying to cash in on the unfortunate events whether for thrill or fame."

"By then we should have more evidence," Connors says already knowing Turnbow's response.

"*Should* is the operative word, Liam," Turnbow says and raises his brow. "I'll need to have sufficient evidence in hand before I can in good conscience file four first degree murder charges. The courts frown on prosecutors who file charges that are considered groundless, frivolous, and vexatious. Keep in mind, murder one is a capital offense and ordinarily the proof must be evident and the presumption great to obtain a conviction."

Refusing to let go of the possibility of bringing homicide charges, Lewis asks, "How about a grand jury?"

"Same problem!" Turnbow replies and squints at the two detectives. "I admire your tenacity.

However, *I* would still have a trial to contend with."

"In the interim, Juan is facing a measly misdemeanor leaving the scene of an accident charge and will probably bond out," Lewis says reflectively. And you know what that means!"

"Does Juan know he's a murder suspect?" Turnbow asks.

"He has to know," Lewis says. When we picked him up at his apartment he was informed that," Lewis pauses and looks at Connors, before continuing, "and I quote, 'We have witnesses who claim you may be involved in a string of murders.'" Apparently embarrassed by his having let the cat out of the bag, Connors cringes and scoots lower in his chair. Lewis continues, "With the finger of guilt pointing in his direction, we don't think he'll be hanging around very long. From what we can tell, he has few ties to the community."

Engaging in damage control and trying to ignore the implication that he may have prematurely tipped off their prime suspect, Connors says, "There's a fifth victim, a Samantha McElroy, who our suspected killer has had in his sights who's at risk if he is released. Damn the torpedoes, Ted, how soon can you get this before a grand jury?"

• • •

As luck would have it, the grand jury found

enough evidence to charge. Juan is served with an indictment and arrest warrant. He's sitting in jail with a misdemeanor leaving the scene charge and four felony first degree murder charges.

He now sits in an interrogation room devoid of anything except a steel table and three folding chairs. He takes comfort in the knowledge that the American authorities are more humane than those in Cuba when it comes to extracting information from arrestees and is confident they have nothing on him other than leaving the scene. He waits.

Connors and Lewis keep Juan waiting while they observe his reaction through the two-way mirror embedded in the wall. Apparently, Juan has been on this side of the mirror more than once. He remains calm as he waits. Twenty minutes after his arrest, the detectives enter the interrogation room carrying with them a tape recorder. They take seats across the table from Juan and Connors turns on the tape recorder.

"Juan," Connors begins, "although you're not a citizen of the U.S., you're still entitled to certain rights under the law. We're obliged to advise you of your Constitutional Rights or what is called your *Miranda Rights*, before we question you. Are you aware of that?"

"Yes," says Juan. "I've had them read to me

before."

Connors raises his brow. *I'll just bet you have!* After reading Juan his rights and ascertaining Juan understands them, Connors asks, "Do you wish to waive the presence of an attorney?"

"Absolutely," says Juan. "I ain't done nothin' wrong except leave the scene of an accident 'cause I was scared." Juan takes a long drink from the water bottle sitting on the table.

Lewis leans back in his chair carefully eying Juan. "You're also charged with some other crimes we would like to talk to you about," he says in a casual tone. "They are much more serious than just leaving the scene of an accident. Do you know what I'm talking about?"

"Those other charges are bogus, and you know it. You made 'em up cause you needed someone to pin 'em on. Ain't got nothing to hide," Juan says and squirms in his chair.

"You appear to be nervous," says Connors.

"That's just because I don't want to get deported," replies Juan.

"Can't say I blame you," says Connors. "You can stop the questioning at any time or request the presence of an attorney or both."

"Okay, I know that." Juan says as he leans forward and glares at Connors. After a brief pause, he asks, "Do I need an attorney?"

"Not up to me, Juan. That's your decision."

Juan fidgets a few moments then asks, "You're not blaming me for the deaths of those four women, are you?"

Connors and Lewis exchange glances. "Why do you ask?" Lewis interjects. "Did you know them?"

"Only what I read about them in the newspaper," Juan quickly replies and defiantly folds his arms across his chest and sits back in his chair as if to say *Bring it on!*

"Never dated or went out with any of them?" asks Connors.

"Didn't I just tell you I didn't know them?" Juan says, agitation apparent in his voice. "Wouldn't I know it if I had?"

"If we were to tell you we have witnesses who will testify otherwise," says Connors, "what would you say?"

"I'd say they were all lying and that I better call an attorney before I answer any more questions."

"You can make one call before you are placed in a cell."

"Let me call my boss. I don't have the money to hire an attorney," Juan stammers.

"Want us to call a public defender?"

"Don't trust them. You all work for the government."

"There's a phone on the wall. We'll wait outside while you make that one call."

Outside the presence of Juan, Lewis tells Connors, "He's one cool customer. He doesn't yet know about the typewriter we seized and the other evidence he obviously buried."

Connors nods. "If he hires an attorney and gets ahold of the application for the search warrant, he won't be so cocky," Connors muses. "I don't think his boss, Rusty, is going to bend over backwards to help the little creep."

When Juan ends the call, Connors and Lewis reenter the interrogation room.

"Well!" Connors says.

Looking dejected, Juan says, "Rusty hung up on me."

"Want us to call a public defender?" Lewis again asks.

"Guess I have no choice," Juan smirks.

Soon after making the call to the public defender's office, Deputy State Public Defender Terrance Gleason arrives at the jail. And in light of the seriousness of the impending charges, as expected, Gleason advises his new client to remain silent, at least until after his arraignment.

• • •

It's late morning when they wrap up the interrogation. On his way home, Connors stops by the hospital to check on Evans. The hospital staff is acquainted with Connors and doesn't challenge him when he quietly enters Evans' room. The only sound comes from the array of medical gadgets attached to Evans. As Connors stealthily closes the distance between the door and the hospital bed, he jumps when a voice demands, "Who goes there?"

"Damnit, Jack, you startled me. I thought you were dead..."

"Better...lu...luck next time," Evans slurs. "Tell me, what... happened...after..."

"We got 'em, Jack, thanks to your quick thinking. We caught up with him at his apartment and he consented to a search of his residence. We found the Underwood. D.J. tells us the *e* matches the notes he sent you. A grand jury is expected to return an indictment for the four murders.

"If the rest of the evidence CSI found pans out, we'll have enough to fry his ass four times over. He was a collector, and by the way, Jack, he must've loved your articles, he kept every one of them."

Evans manages a weak smile. Connors didn't offer details. He didn't want to burden Evans with the condition of the items that were buried in the sand and that they may not be admissible as evidence unless they can be connected to the killer.

Evans winces as he says, "Good work..."

Connors watches Evans' eyes slowly close as he falls into a drug-induced sleep. Pulling the sheet up over Evans' chest, Connors whispers, "Couldn't have done it without you." He then slips silently out of the room.

WAVES OF VENGEANCE — JUDITH BLEVINS & CARROLL MULTZ

Chapter Twelve

The Lineup

Sitting on the patio enjoying after-breakfast coffee with Mitch, I open the morning edition of the *Key West Communiqué*. When I read the headline that dominates the frontpage I jump up from my chair. ***ALLEGED SERIAL KILLER IN CUSTODY!***

Mitch is in the midst of swallowing a mouthful of coffee when I scream, "Mitch, they've got him! They've arrested the serial killer."

Mitch chokes, coughs and spews coffee across the table. Taking a handful of paper napkins, he wipes tears from his watering eyes, and sops up the coffee from the table. "That's great news! What… what happened! How'd they get him?"

I read the article to Mitch.

> *Late yesterday the Key West Police Department arrested Juan Santiago in connection with the recent murders of four local women, Carmen Ochoa, Elana Alverez, Marlene Chambers, and Maria Concha.*
>
> *Santiago, a Cuban immigrant, has been working in the U.S. on a green card. At an*

advisement hearing this morning before Judge Renard Livingston, the judge refused to set bail stating: 'Because of the nature of the charges against the defendant and his questionable status, I'm denying bail on the grounds that he's a flight risk and an obvious threat to the community'.

Public defender Terrance Gleason argued that denying Santiago the right to a bond was a violation of his client's constitutional rights. Prosecutor Theodore Turnbow pointed out that the evidence revealed that the defendant was a clear and present danger to the community and that he was a flight risk. The judge then invited defendant's court appointed attorney to take the matter up in the form of a brief if he sought further argument on the matter.

At the conclusion of the hearing, Santiago remains in custody.

Before Mitch and I have a chance to discuss the recent developments, my phone rings. "Hello," I answer.

"Mrs. McElroy, this is Detective Connors. We've made an arrest and would like for you to come down to the jail and view a live lineup."

"Mitch and I just read the article on the front page. And of course, I'll help any way I can." Eager for details, I start to ask, "Can you disclose how—"

Connors interrupts, "I'll fill you in later."

Realizing this was not the time to discuss the details, I say, "When do you want me to appear?" and look at Mitch. He raises his brow leaving the decision up to me.

"This morning if possible…"

I toss the newspaper on the table and stand. "We're on our way," I respond.

• • •

When we arrive at the jail, we're kept waiting in what appears to be an interrogation room. Through the small window in the door, we notice several people come and go before we're summoned in to view the anticipated lineup. Mitch accompanies me into the dark interior of a viewing room. We're seated before a large one-way window. Apparently, we can see in, but the participants in the lineup can't see out.

On the other side of the window, a sheriff's officer comes into view leading five men dressed in jailhouse orange. The five men look amazingly alike and I'm not sure I can pick out the one who assaulted me. Both times that I had contact with him it was dark, and his head was covered with a hood of some sort. The deputy orders the men to step forward one-by-one and to speak a predetermined line.

I rack my brain trying to make a connection. Nothing comes to me and I must admit I cannot honestly say it was any one of them.

At the conclusion of the lineup, the suspects are taken back to their respective jail cells and Detective Connors enters. "Anyone in the lineup look familiar?"

"Sorry to say," I reply. "They all look like him. I can't say for sure if any of them was my assailant."

Connors nods. "We've had other witnesses view the lineup and a couple were able to tentatively identify one in particular as someone they had seen with a victim. However, that in and of itself, doesn't go very far in a murder prosecution. Being seen with someone doesn't make one a murderer."

I've been eagerly awaiting details of the arrest. When Connors doesn't volunteer, I say, "Ah, you were going to fill us in."

"Of course," Connors replies. "We apprehended the suspect when we received a lead from a potential witness. The lead led us to his place of employment and his employer identified him mainly from the red paint smear."

"Oh, my," I say.

"Yes. And thanks to you for observing it when you were attacked. That bit of information has been invaluable." Connors then stands, signifying we're free to leave, he says, "Thanks for coming down. We'll be in touch."

On the way home, Mitch says, "We should have brought Attila. He'd been able to pick the bastard out of the lineup with just one sniff."

I nod. "But then again, having a dog hate you doesn't make you a murderer—as Detective Connors so eloquently stated."

. . .

Later that day, Lewis and Connors meet in Connors' office. "Jim," Connors says, "we're gonna need more than the typewriter and items that we can't prove he ever had possession of to get a conviction. Too bad we didn't discover the tennis shoes with the paint at his residence. Almost all the witnesses mentioned that particular piece of evidence." After a pause, Connors adds, "I was thinking of photographing the other items we found in the brush and do a house-to-house to see if we can come up with something."

"I'm game. How'd you suggest we proceed?" Lewis asks.

"You're familiar with the route Santiago ran when he bolted. Perhaps you could cover that area while I show the photos of the other items around. The ring, even though inexpensive, is gaudy and appears to be unique. Maybe a jeweler could identify it."

Having planned their strategy, the next day Connors and Lewis embark on their designated missions. Lewis literally goes from door-to-door along the route he figured Juan had taken to get to the apartment building before the police arrived. By midday, he was feeling discouraged as no one remembered seeing a stranger running through their neighborhood on the day in question.

Lewis, growing weary, meanders down the street where Bethany Olgesby lives. Bethany is once again in her rose garden coddling her roses. Upon spotting Bethany, Lewis approaches. "Afternoon, ma'am," he chirps.

"And to you, as well," she responds. "Can I help you locate an address? You appear to be lost."

Lewis notices the lady has a tight grip on the pruning shears as if to be prepared to fend off an attack. Not wanting to upset her, he immediately takes his badge from his pocket and introduces himself.

The lady closely examines Lewis' police badge, and then looking up into his face, says, "I'm Bethany Olgesby and I'm glad to meet you. One can't be too careful these days, you know." After lowering the pruning shears to a less threatening position, she removes her gloves and says, "Why, just the other day I was working in my roses when a strange man appeared from out of nowhere. He stopped by the dumpster over there," and she points with the pruning shears, "pulled off his shoes, tossed them into the dumpster, and then ran off in that direction barefooted," pointing again with the shears. "Very strange indeed."

Before Lewis could comment, Bethany rushes on. "Sammy must've seen the whole thing. He immediately approached the dumpster and retrieved the shoes. My word! Even though one of them was ruined with red paint, he put them on and danced around like he'd won the lottery."

Lewis' heartbeat increased. *Paydirt!* When he was finally able to get a word in, he asked, "Who is Sammy?"

"Oh, Colonel Samuel Culpepper, also known as Sammy, he's one of our local vagrants. He prowls the neighborhood going through trash. I feel sorry for him. He appears to be demented and constantly talks to himself." Then, with a sanctimonious expression, Bethany says, "I keep him supplied with my homemade chocolate chip cookies."

"Most kind of you," Lewis says as he looks

down the street. "Where does Sammy live?" he asks.

"Don't know for sure if he has a home. The only time I see him is when he comes by to pick up the cookies and go through the dumpster."

"Does he have a regular routine?" Lewis asks.

"He usually shows up the mornings before the trash is collected," Bethany replies.

"And when might that be?" Lewis asks.

"Let's see, today's Thursday—tomorrow morning."

"Would you be able to identify the stranger if need be?" Lewis asks.

"Don't know. I didn't get a good look at his face. I think he might be of Cuban descent, almost as tall as the dumpster and has a muscular build."

Lewis records Bethany's name, address, and phone number in his notebook. "Thank you, Ms. Oglesby. You've been extremely helpful."

"You're welcome, officer. Now, I have a question for you. Does this have anything to do with the arrest of the serial killer?" she asks.

"Very well could be, ma'am." Lewis notices a look of shock on Bethany's face and quickly adds, "We have a suspect in custody and you're not in any danger, ma'am. I'll probably see you tomorrow morning."

• • •

After Lewis left Connors' office to start canvassing his territory, Connors checked the phonebook and made a list of jewelers along with their addresses. Before long, Connors was pounding the pavement going from jeweler to jeweler, showing the photograph of the diamond ring hoping someone will recognize it. When he enters *Bling Boutique*, the third store on his list, he's greeted by a gum-chewing clerk with purple hair and pink braces on her teeth. The clerk's nametag identifies her as Kitty. The interior of the store is stocked with racks of inexpensive costume jewelry of every variety, the kind that appeals to teenagers. A sign displayed on the wall behind a glass counter advertises: *If the ring has no bling, then it don't mean a thing!*

Kitty notices Connors looking at the sign, and pointing to it, says, "Pretty cute, huh? Made it up myself."

"Catchy," replies Connors and shows Kitty his badge.

Kitty's attitude changes from flamboyant to serious. She pales as she asks, "Am I in trouble?"

"Why, did you do something?" Connors asks.

"Only a little weed…" Kitty replies.

"I'll give you a pass," Connors quips. He then

pulls the photo of the ring from a folder he has tucked under his arm. "Does the ring depicted in this photo look familiar?"

"Umm, it could be one of ours, why?"

"Can't disclose the details. It's part of an ongoing investigation. So, I'll ask you again, do you recognize it?"

Kitty then studies the photo more closely, "Yes," she says. "We used to carry a line called *Almost the Real Thing.* However, when the products started being returned by angry customers, the boss nixed 'em. They were pretty cheap and looked good for only a few months."

"Do you remember selling this particular style to anyone about five months ago?"

"As a matter of fact, I do remember a guy coming in about that time. I was gettin' ready to close when he showed up. Said he just got off work. He smelled like fish and I almost gagged. He was all full of himself. Said he was going to marry the most beautiful girl in the world, and he wanted the biggest stone in the store. When I showed him that one or one like it, he went bananas." Kitty points to the photo of the ring, "That style is so gaudy, we really didn't sell very many of 'em—guess that's why I remember."

Connors asks, "Did he pay by cash or credit

card?"

"It was only fifty dollars and he paid cash."

"Remember what he looked like?"

Most likely being relieved she isn't the target of the investigation, Kitty is quick to respond. "Big, dark hair and eyes, very muscular," she says. "He in trouble?"

Connors ignores her question and extracts a photo lineup from the folder. The lineup features six photos of young men with similar facial features and coloring. He places it on the counter. "Does anyone in this lineup look like the guy?"

Kitty takes her time studying the photos. "Five months is a long time…all these guys look so much alike, I can't be sure."

Connors nods. He then takes Kitty's name, address and phone number. "Thanks for your help. Here's my card, call me if you remember anything," he says as he prepares to leave. "By the way, take it easy on that weed, it can get you in trouble."

Connors reflects on the physical lineup where the surviving target was unable to positively identify her attacker. *Damn!* Connors thinks as he walks to the parking lot. The laws regarding lineups require that they can't be suggestive—otherwise, any resulting identification will be deemed tainted and inadmissible in court. *So much for picking photographs that closely resemble the suspect.*

· · ·

Lewis returns to the neighborhood where he interviewed Bethany early the day before. He takes up a position on the opposite side of the street from where the dumpster is located so as not to scare Sammy away. Not long into his wait, he sees a raggedy elderly man moseying down the street. It appears he's muttering to himself and occasionally gestures with his hands. When the man stops at the dumpster, Lewis approaches him.

"Mornin', Sammy."

Sammy jerks around. "Twern't doin' nuttin," he stammers. "Just lookin' for sumptin to eat."

"Easy, old-timer. How 'bout I buy you breakfast at a café in town?" Lewis offers.

Sammy squints at Lewis and then looks down at his raggedy attire. "Not fit for no café," he says. "McDonald's?"

"Come on, let's go," Lewis replies and escorts Sammy to his vehicle.

Over breakfast of egg McMuffins and coffee, Lewis interviews Sammy. Sammy's story of finding the shoes squares with Bethany's to the letter. As they leave the restaurant and walk toward the car, Lewis asks, "What'd you do with the shoes you found?"

"Oh, they too tight, hurt my feet. I got 'em ta home in a place where's I can see 'em."

"Would you show them to me?" Lewis asks.

"Shore!" Sammy says, and the pride in his voice is unmistakable.

Lewis drives Sammy to his *home* which consists of a small tent located at the corner of a vacant lot. *This is going to change as soon as I can arrange it,* Lewis thinks as he pulls up in front of the tent.

"You wanna come in?" Sammy asks, looking somewhat embarrassed.

The tent is barely large enough for one man, much less two. "Naw, I'll wait here," Lewis replies. "Okay, I'll bring 'em out." Sammy says as he disappears inside the tent.

When Sammy is out of sight, Lewis extracts five twenty-dollar bills from his wallet, folds them in a neat bundle and drops them out of the car window in plain sight.

Moments later Sammy's back carrying the shoes. "Here they be," he says and smiles broadly. The shoes were an exact match to the descriptions of the witnesses. "Sammy, would you let me have these shoes?" Lewis asks.

Sammy draws back. The look on his face says he's ready to fight. "Nope! They's mine, I done found 'em, fair an square."

Lewis reasons that if Sammy hasn't been wearing the shoes, there may still be some of Juan's DNA left in the footbeds. He knows that he could legally confiscate them to use as evidence in a murder trial if need be, but he would only do that as a last resort.

Sammy, standing beside the vehicle, is close enough for Lewis to look into his eyes. "Funny thing, Sammy," Lewis says, "while I was waiting for you, I spotted some cash laying right there on the ground. You must've dropped it when you got out of the car," Lewis says and points to the money. Sammy looks down and seeing the money for the first time, says, "'Taint mine."

"Well, taint mine either," Lewis says. "Since there's only two of us present, it has to be yours." Sammy picks up the cash and his eyes grow wide, "A hundred dollars!"

"How 'bout you take the cash and I take the shoes?"

"Hell, yes," Sammy blurts. His look conveys that Sammy knows what Lewis is up to. He hands the shoes to Lewis through the open car window. Without saying another word, with cash in hand, Sammy turns and shuffles back toward his tent.

Realizing he didn't get any identifying

information from Sammy, Lewis reflects that Sammy has no address or phone number to speak of anyway. All he has to call his own is the name Colonel Samuel Culpepper—and chances are that may not even be legit.

• • •

When Connors calls me with an update on the lack of any positive identification with the various witnesses, I don't feel like the klutz I consider myself to be when I was unable to identify my attacker. Mitch made sure of that even before Connors made the call.

"Your attacker apparently had no distinguishing features," Mitch says. "Such as a visible scar, tattoo or physical deformity. One of my dad's law partners, as you know, does criminal defense and says if the lineup is unduly suggestive, identification of the defendant at trial by a so-called eyewitness will be disallowed. In other words, if only one of the participants in the lineup has long blond hair and a full beard fitting the description of the perpetrator it will be deemed to be an improper lineup. In your case, it looks like the police did too good of a job in their collection of matches for their composite."

"I was too busy defending myself, and as I look back, my attacker never really exposed his face. Out on the beach he had a hood of some kind and at the house something very similar."

"Sam, don't beat yourself up. When one of my golfing buddies who had been a federal prosecutor was robbed at gunpoint and asked if the robber had a mustache, and despite the fact they had been eyeball to eyeball, had to admit he didn't know. That's why, according to my dad's law partner, eyewitness testimony is not as good as circumstantial evidence such as DNA and fingerprints."

Chapter Thirteen

The Evidence

After they complete their missions, Lewis and Connors meet in Connors' office to compare notes. Lewis has already tagged the tennis shoes and placed them with the evidence custodian and asked D.J. to examine them for DNA.

After they're settled in Connors' office, Lewis goes first. He tells Connors, in detail, the events of his morning's encounter.

"Colonel Samuel Culpepper!" quips Connors. "You gotta be kidding…"

"Nope, that's his name alright. However, he goes by Sammy. Lewis even does a good job, at least in his opinion, of imitating Sammy's *English*. He concludes by saying, he's been around the block a few times and he's your typical hard-luck story. But don't underestimate him, he's sharp as a tack."

At the conclusion of Lewis' narration, Connors says, "I didn't fare as well as you." He then tells Lewis about finding the curio shop where he suspects Santiago bought the ring. "The clerk's a pothead. She couldn't pick our boy out of the photo lineup. However, she did say the purchaser bragged that he was going to marry the most beautiful girl in the world… and, oh yes, and then scrunching up her noise, added, he smelled like fish."

"Smelling like fish isn't an uncommon trait in this neck of the woods," Lewis comments.

"Right you are," replies Connors just as his phone rings. "Connors," he answers.

"Liam, this is D.J. Is Lewis with you?"

"Sitting right here. What's up?" Connors asks.

"We were able to get two samples of DNA from the footbeds of the shoes. As you well know, in order to identify them, we'll need specimens from the folks who wore the shoes," D.J. says.

Giving Lewis a thumbs-up, Connors replies, "We're on it." After ending the call, Connors says to Lewis, "D.J. found DNA in the footbeds. We need samples from Santiago and Sammy. Can't see Santiago voluntarily giving a sample so I'll contact the DA and have him obtain a court order authorizing the collection of DNA samples. That way Juan won't have a choice."

"While you're doing that, I'll round up Sammy and bring him in to supply a sample of his DNA," says Lewis. "Don't think he'll buck at the idea, especially if I throw in a Big Mac."

Before the detectives leave Connors' office the phone rings again. Connors answers.

"Liam, you hung up so fast I didn't get a chance to tell you the rest," says D.J.

"Okay, Lewis is still here. I'm going to put you on speaker." A moment later Connors says, "Okay, we're ready."

"This morning when we examined the hairclip, we found several strands of hair tangled in the clip. The DNA matched victim number two, Marlene Chambers," D.J. says. "And some skin cells obtained from the chain attached to the little gold cross contained DNA from victim number three, Elana Alverez. We also found the initials EA inscribed on the back of the cross. They're pretty faint having been eroded from years of wear I suspect but were still visible, but just barely."

Connors and Lewis reach across Connors' desk and exchange a high five.

After a long pause, D.J. asks, "You there, Liam?"

"Yes, we're here. Damn good work, D.J."

• • •

Turnbow is just returning from a hearing when Connors enters the courthouse. They meet in the corridor. "Hey, Liam," Turnbow says. "You here to see me?"

"I am. It appears that things are looking up. D.J. traced some strands of hair from the hairclip to Marlene Chambers and DNA from the gold cross was traced back to Elana Alverez along with the initials *EA* inscribed on the back."

"What! That's great news—" Turnbow blurts.

"That's not all. We recovered the tennis shoes, and D.J. found DNA in the footbeds. We need a court order to collect DNA from Santiago."

"Christmas in July! I needed some good news after the contentious hearing I was just drug through." Turnbow comments.

"Did you win?" Connors asks.

"The evidence was on our side and we won the battle. However, the war is still pending. Come on into my office," Turnbow beckons.

After they complete the request form, Connors sets out to find a judge to get it signed. Since there are several judges in the courthouse, finding one wasn't that difficult. In less than an hour, Connors has a court order in hand for Juan Santiago ordering him to comply with the request for non-testimonial identification. Connors contacts Terrance Gleason, Juan's attorney, and informs him he's on his way to the jail to serve the order. Gleason replies saying he'll meet Connors at the jail.

• • •

Juan looks surprised when he sees Connors and the jailhouse nurse approach his cell. Gleason, his court appointed attorney is right behind them.

"What…what's going on?" Juan asks and looks past Connors to Gleason, apparently expecting an answer from his attorney.

"We have a court order to obtain a sample of your DNA," Connors says without giving Gleason an opportunity to respond. "Nurse Lambert is here to collect the sample."

Juan is on his feet protesting. Grabbing the bars on his cell, he shouts, "No! I don't have to—"

Gleason intervenes, "They have a valid court order, Juan, so, yes, you do have to submit, either voluntarily or otherwise."

Juan sags and doesn't put up any resistance when Nurse Lambert swabs samples of saliva from his mouth.

• • •

It's late morning and Lewis hopes to find Sammy in his tent in the vacant lot. As he traverses the streets, Lewis sees Sammy walking in the direction of his usual haunts. Lewis honks and when Sammy turns, Lewis waves at him. Sammy stops curbside and waits. When Lewis gets close enough, he calls out the open driver's window, "Where you off to?"

Sammy saunters over to the car. "Oh, thought I'd pick up some cookies from Mrs. Oglesby and check out the dumpster," he says. "'Twernt that long ago I found some prize shoes."

"So you did," Lewis replies. "As it turns out, the shoes you found may have belonged to a person we've been looking for."

Sammy looks perplexed. "But, I done already give ya the shoes."

"Yes, you did. And it's obvious the other person wore the shoes before getting rid of them. We now need to know how many others wore the shoes. That we can determine through DNA testing."

"Unh huh," Sammy says, and Lewis notices suspicion leap into Sammy's eyes. "What ya need from me?" Sammy asks.

"A sample of your DNA to compare to the samples the lab found in the footbeds of the shoes so we can eliminate you and focus on the one who placed them in the dumpster."

Before Sammy can respond, their attention is diverted when they hear the sound of a garbage truck approaching. Sammy looks up the street toward the dumpster. He's obviously disappointed that he's missed an opportunity to claim any prizes before the trash is picked up, Sammy grumbles, "Done give a sample at the VA last week. Can't ya use that one?"

"Ah, we need to obtain a blood or saliva specimen in our laboratory under controlled conditions because it could be used as evidence in a criminal prosecution."

Sammy looks toward the dumpster which is in the process of being emptied. He then looks back at Lewis and says, "Okay," but grudgingly adds, "Glad ta 'blige."

• • •

After visiting the crime lab at the police department where Sammy's saliva sample is collected, Lewis swings into a McDonald's on the way back to Sammy's neighborhood.

"How about a Big Mac and some fries?" Lewis asks as he pulls into a parking slot.

"Shore!" Sammy blurts and opens the passenger door. Sammy is almost inside the restaurant before Lewis clears the car. *He's certainly eager.*

It's between lunch and dinner so the restaurant is virtually empty. "You grab us a table and I'll get the order," Lewis says. "Coke or Sprite?"

"Don't matter, I'm not picky," Sammy replies as he heads for a table by the windows.

Conversation is sparse, and as Sammy eats like there's no tomorrow, Lewis studies him closely. About halfway through the meal, Sammy quits eating, wraps the rest of his burger, and puts it in a paper bag along with the remaining fries.

Bewildered, Lewis asks, "What's up, partner.

Didn't you like the sandwich?"

"Like it fine. Savin' part for supper," Sammy says and wipes his lips with a paper napkin.

"Whoa! We'll get you one to go. You go ahead and finish this one," Lewis coaxes. Confused as to why Sammy is so hungry after having given him money a few days before, Lewis asks, "Did you lose the money?"

"Nope! Give it to widow lady. She got two kids…"

Lewis is now looking at Sammy with deeper admiration. Sammy has nothing to call his own and when he does get a windfall, he compassionately gives it to a more needy person. "Sammy, she can probably get public assistance—"

"She too proud. And 'sides, says she don't know how," Sammy murmurs.

"Well, I know how. Where does she live? I'll send a social worker out to interview her as soon as this afternoon."

Sammy perks up, "You can do that?"

"Damn straight, and since you're a vet, there are programs that can help you, too," Lewis says.

After lunch, Lewis drops Sammy off at his tent and heads back to the office. *Sammy's the kind of person you don't mind helping!* thinks Lewis as a broad smile crosses his face.

Nurse Lambert delivers Juan's saliva sample to the crime lab upon their return from the jail. A few minutes later, Lewis arrives, and he and Connors meet in Connors' office to compare notes.

"How'd Psycho-man react to having to comply with the court order requiring non-testimonial identification?" Lewis asks.

"He balked, but Gleason convinced him otherwise. The nurse maintained the chain of custody and took the sample to the lab. D.J. should have some results to us by the end of the day." Connors pauses before asking, "How'd it go on your end?"

"Without a hitch. Took Sammy to the lab, they collected a sample. Later, we went to lunch and then I took Sammy home. Piece-o-cake!"

Connors taps his ballpoint on the pile of papers stacking up in his In-basket. "I should tackle some of this but I'm much too antsy to concentrate. Wanna hit the gym and play some handball while we wait?"

"Hell yes! It always buoys my spirits to beat the pants off you."

"Ha! You wish! Put your money where your mouth is," Connors says, and the two of them head for the gym.

Halfway through the second game, Connors' cellphone rings. He rushes to answer it. "Yes!"

"D.J. here. We've finished the testing. It appears that your suspect left a substantial amount of DNA on the footbeds of the shoes."

Connors gives Lewis a thumbs up and asks D.J., "Find any other DNA?"

"Only a small amount from the vagrant Lewis brought in earlier today," D.J. answers.

"Thanks for expediting the process," Connors says to D.J. "We need to nail this SOB as soon as possible before the public nails our hide to the wall."

D.J. laughs. "Any time, my friend, any time."

Back in the locker room, Connors says to Lewis as they change, "Looks like the worm is turning—and in our favor. D.J. is sending over the report as we speak. You want to accompany me as I deliver copies to Gleason and Turnbow?"

"Wouldn't miss it for the world!" Lewis says, as he finishes tying his shoelaces. "One won't be very happy, the other ecstatic."

Chapter Fourteen

Pathway to Trial

"Why so glum, chum?" Mitch asks. "Someone steal your bubblegum?"

"Wondering why charges were filed in the death of four lookalikes but not in my case," I snap.

"Easy answer," Mitch says, "other than the red paint on the tennis shoe you observed, there's nothing to indicate Juan was your attacker—only speculation. Since you couldn't identify your attacker, anyone could've worn Juan's shoes at the time of the two attacks. That's assuming, of course, no one else ever spilled red paint on their shoes."

I'm disappointed in Mitch's comment. "I thought you were in my corner," I say.

"I am," he replies and reaches for my hand.

"Doesn't look like it to me!" I say and pull away.

"Sam, place yourself in the position of a jury that would hear the case or better yet place yourself in Juan's position. If you were the one being charged, and were innocent, would you want to be convicted on such flimsy evidence?" After a brief pause, he finishes. "I'm only trying to be a realist."

I analyze Mitch's racialization and reign in my disappointment. "You make a good point. However, deep inside I know Juan's not innocent."

"From my scanty knowledge of the law, that's not the gauge. Not sure there's even enough evidence to convict Juan on the murder charges. If he's found not guilty, according to my business law professor in college who was a former criminal defense attorney, once he's been placed in jeopardy he can't be tried again no matter what evidence later is discovered."

"Did I hear you right? You mean if the authorities later find an eyewitness or Juan's fingerprints or DNA to tie him to the murders, he can't be retried?"

"Exactly! Even if Juan confesses, he can't be retried. So, holding back on prosecuting the bastard for having assaulted you is not such a bad idea until they have better evidence connecting him to the murders. Otherwise, he dodges five bullets and is given a free pass to kill again or at least attempt to do so."

"Maybe the authorities will get lucky!" I say. "According to Connors, the follow-up investigation often turns up valuable information."

"Right now, our main aim is to keep you safe. Whether a conviction or not, anyone and everyone who bears any resemblance to the victims must be protected."

"Maybe I should dye my hair, put on a few pounds, and start wearing glasses and no makeup," I say only half serious.

"Mitch glares at me. "You do and I'll tear up our marriage license."

"And if it saves my life?"

"Then I'll start feeding you milkshakes, burgers and fries and a lot of them."

"How about bon-bons?"

"Them, too!" he says in a tone that conveys the unmistakable message, don't even think about it!

Our laugh bespeaks of frustration and Mitch holds me tightly in his arms. This time, I don't pull away.

• • •

Connors and Lewis are busy mulling over their reports in preparation for trial. Normally, investigating officers are not allowed to read from their reports while testifying. Often, the only thing standing in the way of a conviction is either an ineffective investigation, ineffective testimony in court or a combination of the two. Eager to obtain a conviction that will withstand an appeal, the two labor feverishly. It's apparent that, in their opinion, an acquittal is not an acceptable option!

They're interrupted by the receptionist's announcement that Kitty Taylor is on the phone and says it is important to speak with Officer Connors.

"Detective Connors here," Connors answers.

"This is Kitty Taylor from *Bling Boutique*. You told me to call if I had any other information concerning the purchase of one of our artificial diamonds."

"Yes, I remember Ms. Taylor," says Connors. "How can I assist you?"

"When you asked about our surveillance cameras, I told you the tape had been replaced and the old one disposed of. Well, I was told by the firm that services the cameras that the old ones are kept for a year and not immediately destroyed. I located the tape for the date I sold the fake diamond to the person you asked about and have it here. I have permission from the owner of *Bling* to turn it over to you."

Looking at Lewis, Connors replies, "Detective Lewis and I are on our way."

• • •

With the help of the tape, Connors and Lewis receive the break they've been looking for. On the date of the sale of the ring, standing at the front of the display case in full view of one of the cameras is Juan. Connors and Lewis watch as Juan examines the ring and fanning out a number of bills he retrieved from his wallet, hands them to Kitty. It also looks as though Juan is handing Kitty something else along with the bills. Curious as to what Juan pulled from his wallet in addition to the bills, Connors asks, "You say the purchaser didn't pay by credit card. What was it he handed to you and that you promptly returned?"

"It was a photo of the girl he said he was buying the ring for— 'the most beautiful woman in the world.'" Says Kitty with a frown. "Why do you ask?"

"Ever see the woman before?"

"No, I just took a quick glance but long enough to wonder what she saw in him."

"Think you would recognize her photograph?"

"Maybe."

With that Lewis retrieves the newspaper composite of the four murder victims from a folder and shows the composite to Kitty.

"That's her," Kitty says excitedly as she points to Carmen Ochoa. "She's wearing a set of earrings similar to the ones I wear." With that Kitty pulls her purple hair to the side exposing earrings similar to the ones worn by Carmen Ochoa. "My parents gave me these when I graduated from high school," she says. "They're the real thing, not the kind of junk we sell here."

"How come you didn't tell us all this before?" Connors asks.

Kitty shrugs, "Because you never asked me nor showed me her picture before."

"Her picture has been in all the newspapers," says Lewis.

"I don't read the newspaper. Our local newspaper is all ads, and I don't watch the news on television anymore because it's all slanted."

• • •

Armed with the latest, Connors and Lewis head for the DA's office. "You two look like the cat that swallowed the canary," Turnbow says. "Jessica tells me you couldn't wait until our meeting tomorrow." Turnbow raises his brow as he pushes aside the file he's been working on as if to say, "the interruption better be damn well worth it!"

Connors rudely slings the supplemental report containing the newly discovered evidence onto Turnbow's desk. "Maybe this will change your disposition," he says in a tone harsher than he intended. That Connors is not one of Turnbow's most avid supporters is an understatement. *Turnbow is a prima donna who thinks he's a god just because he has a juris doctor degree. Maybe we need to address him as Your Eminence since we're peons—at least in his estimation.*

There has always been a tug-of-war between some cops and some DAs. The DAs complain about the egos of the cops and the cops complain about the egos of the DA's. Both complain about the egos of judges.

As Turnbow reads the supplemental report, a smile crosses his face. He turns the pages of the report over to see if there is anything written on the backside. That is usually Turnbow's way of saying, "Is this all there is?" But not this time. "Great work!" he finally says to Connors and Lewis. "This may be what spells the difference between a conviction and an acquittal."

WAVES OF VENGEANCE — JUDITH BLEVINS & CARROLL MULTZ

Chapter Fifteen

The Trial

Hush spreads over the crowded courtroom as Juan is ushered in accompanied by two deputy sheriffs. He's led to a table identified by a nameplate indicating *Defense*. Terrance Gleason, the head public defender, together with an assistant by the name of Jayden Greene, greet Juan with handshakes. Well-groomed and wearing a shirt and tie, Juan looks every bit the part of a recent college graduate on his way to a job interview.

Turnbow is seated at a similar table identified by a nameplate indicating *Prosecution* along with assistant district attorney Rachel Fleming. Also seated at the prosecution table is Detective Liam Connors who has been designated as the prosecution's advisory witness.

"Juan just smiled at me," Rachel whispers to Turnbow sounding like a schoolgirl.

Looking irritated by the interruption, Turnbow glances up from his notes, and says, "You do look a little bit like the victims in this case. He may be earmarking you for *seis*, number six. That is as soon as he polishes off *cuatro*, his original number four.

He's had two runs at her, and you know what they say, 'Third time's the charm!'" Turnbow watches Rachel turn pale under the harsh overhead lights in the courtroom.

"Not funny," Rachel says and grimaces. "You don't think—"

"Of course not. That's just incentive for you to stay on your toes and help me convict this SOB," Turnbow whispers.

Within minutes Judge Renard Livingston's entry is heralded by an announcement by the bailiff that the court is in session.

After the preliminaries, the tedious task of selecting twelve unbiased residents of the community to be jurors begins. Since Turnbow is asking for the death penalty, much time is taken, maybe more than necessary, to sort out those who are irrevocably committed against imposition of the death penalty. "An inhuman penalty even for a serial killer," several of the prospective jurors declare. Outside the courthouse two groups of protestors clash, one opposing the death penalty, the other chanting, "Death to the serial killer."

"I'm damned if I do and damned if I don't," Turnbow whispers to Rachel. "If we obtain a conviction and the death penalty, we're going to alienate a lot of people. And if we obtain a conviction and no death penalty, the victims' families and their friends will want my ouster."

"What happens if we don't end up with either?" Rachel whispers back, apparently remembering their earlier conversation and that Juan could be exonerated.

"Then call Phillip's Mortuary. For many, an acquittal will be considered an unforgivable sin and of course the fault of the DA. Never mind the quantity or quality of the evidence."

Rachel replies, "At least one jury, the grand jury, has already found enough evidence to charge. Maybe this one will find enough evidence to convict."

"One could only hope!" Turnbow says as Judge Livingston glares at him and gives him the universal sign to be silent.

The opening statement is the opportunity for each side to outline the evidence they expect to present. Although the defense is not required to present evidence, they usually do so. The same is true with respect to a defendant who's not required by law to testify. However, usually they do. In a murder prosecution, the jury wants the defendant to take the stand and proclaim his or her innocence in plain and unambiguous language. Without denial, there is usually a conviction.

The jury ultimately selected was not to Turnbow's liking, however, it was one both he and Rachel thought they could live with. They really had no choice. Ordinarily, it was the luck of the draw anyway. Some jurors are almost as good as attorneys at framing their narratives to fit their agenda—a desire to serve or not serve.

• • •

Turnbow gave the opening statement for the prosecution. "Ladies and gentlemen of the jury," he began. We are now at that stage of the trial where the attorneys have the opportunity to make opening statements as to what they think the evidence will show and to present a sneak preview of their case.

"The evidence we present will show that four young women washed ashore on the beaches of Key West within a short span of time. Not only did it appear all four were drowned, but that all shared a common trait—they all looked alike. Their deaths appeared to have been by accidental drowning except for the fact that no one reported them as having drowned and more importantly all four had bruising indicating they had been in some type of altercation before their deaths.

"The evidence will show the Defendant was involved in a relationship with the first victim, Carmen Ochoa. In fact, Defendant, at or about the time of Carmen's death, purchased an artificial diamond engagement ring from a local store here in Key West that specialized in costume jewelry. While the clerk, Kitty Taylor, waited on the defendant and sold him the artificial diamond ring, she wasn't sure the purchaser was the defendant until she viewed a video of the transaction. She will testify that during the purchase, the Defendant showed her a photograph of the person for whom he claimed the ring was purchased, Carmen Ochoa. Ms. Taylor recognized a newspaper photograph of Carmen and will testify that the two photographs were of the same person.

"When the Defendant was arrested and his apartment and surrounding area searched, evidence connecting him to the four deaths was discovered. The search of the landscape at the apartment complex revealed a recently dug hole in the sand under a clump of foliage. When excavated, the hole yielded the following items: the artificial diamond ring purchased for victim number one, Carmen Ochoa; a gold cross with the initials *EA* we contend belonged to victim number two, Elana Alverez; a hair clip later determined to contain strands of hair originating from victim number three, Marlene Chambers; and a Sigma Delta sorority charm bracelet containing the DNA of victim number four, Maria Concha. Also recovered from the hiding place were newspaper clippings that had been extracted from our local newspaper relating to the deaths of the four women lookalikes.

"In addition to the above items, which we will introduce into evidence, will be an Underwood typewriter seized from Defendant's apartment. It, as one of our forensic experts will testify, contains a defective key. Not just any key but one of the vowels—the letter *e*. Why is that important? Because the typed notes sent by the killer to the newspaper bragging about each of the killings had the same defective typewritten letter. The actual notes bragging about the killings, we contend were sent by the Defendant, will also be introduced into evidence.

"Also tying the Defendant to the killings is a pair of tennis shoes that contained the Defendant's DNA. A witness will testify a man matching Defendant's description, was seen by her running down the street. The witness will testify the person removed the shoes, including the one with red paint stains, threw them into a dumpster, and ran away barefooted. The witness who observed the abandonment of the shoes is an elderly lady by the name of Bethany Oglesby. The same witness will testify that within minutes, a homeless man whom she knew as Colonel Samuel Culpepper retrieved the shoes from the dumpster. Colonel Samuel Culpepper will testify he turned over the same pair of shoes to the authorities. Those shoes will be introduced into evidence.

"Why are the tennis shoes important you may ask? Because several of our witnesses will testify they saw a man matching Defendant's description with various victims prior to their deaths—a man wearing a pair of tennis shoes with red paint stains. Defendant's prior employer, Rusty Dugan, owner of Dugan's Fish Distributors, will testify he was with Defendant when the Defendant spilled the red paint on his shoes.

"After all the evidence is presented, the only logical conclusion will be that the Defendant was involved in all four deaths, and therefore, guilty on all four murder charges and that justice cries out for convictions."

• • •

Mitch attended the trial but thought it best that I not be present. According to Mitch and Detectives Connors and Lewis, it would only fuel the fire.

"Your presence would give Juan another reason to add you to the list," Mitch said.

"And could very well taint your identification, should the occasion arise," Connors said.

Mitch did give me a blow by blow account of Juan's trial. He said he was impressed by Turnbow's handling of the case thus far.

"Do you think Gleason will give an opening statement now or wait until after the prosecution's case has been concluded?" I ask Mitch.

"I'm no expert, but if the defense waits, the jury may already have made up its mind and no amount of evidence presented to the contrary will be able to change it," Mitch says. "In other words, the defense can't risk waiting to let the jury be swayed without letting them know there's another side to the case."

This is a side of Mitch I hadn't seen before, and I'm impressed with how much he knows about trials. But then again both his father and grandfather were trial lawyers.

"How in the world can Juan squirm out of this one?" I ask.

"You'd be surprised," Mitch replies. "Appears he's conned a lot of people before reaching this stage in his life."

"Are you saying you think he will be taking the stand in his own behalf?"

"Hell, yes! He has nothing to lose and will be lying his ass off."

"Guess we'll find out after Gleason's opening statement. Too bad I can't be there to listen."

"Good morning, ladies and gentlemen. My name is Terrance Gleason. I represent Juan Santiago, the Defendant in this case.

"Although a defendant is never required to testify or prove his innocence, the Defendant in this case will. First, he will deny he had anything to do with the death of any of the women. As a man about town and being new in the area, he met a lot of women. Intrigued by the sea, he gravitated to women who spent a lot of time enjoying the ocean. When he met Carmen Ochoa, one of the named victims in this case, the two fell in love and he proposed to her after several dates.

"The night after he proposed, Carmen Ochoa stood him up, or at least so he thought. Learning about her death, while watching a local TV channel, he was devastated.

"Mr. Santiago contends the police, after allegedly finding an engagement ring, a gold cross with the initials EA, a hair clip and a Sigma Delta sorority charm bracelet in bushes near his apartment building, decided they needed a fall guy—someone to blame for what could very well have been accidental drownings. What's to say those items weren't planted there by the police after they were removed from the bodies and after Mr.

Santiago became a suspect.

"Although a lot of Cubans fit his general description, Juan will testify he's not sure why the authorities zeroed in on him. Maybe perhaps because of his relationship with Carmen Ochoa.

"As for the newspaper articles allegedly found by the police in the shrubs outside his apartment building, he will deny that he clipped those articles or any articles from the newspaper and placed them there. He did not have a subscription to the newspaper and seldom read the newspapers. He contends the articles were placed there by the police along with the other items in their quest to frame him.

"Now, as for the Underwood typewriter allegedly found in his apartment at the same time as the items in the bushes. He will testify that he doesn't know where the typewriter came from; that he never learned to type; that his language and writing skills weren't of the level found in the notes; and that all the forms he fills out and letters he composes are handwritten. He will contend that he never used the typewriter and if he had his fingerprints would have been on the keyboard.

"As for the pair of tennis shoes found in a dumpster some distance from where Juan lived, he will testify that he threw those out when he purchased a new pair—the pair he's wearing in court today. He will testify the old pair was badly stained with paint from a painting project at work and were discarded in a dumpster behind his apartment building and not in the dumpster where they were later claimed to have been found.

"If the evidence is as we anticipate, we will have no hesitancy at the conclusion of the evidence in asking that you return not guilty verdicts on all charges. Not because we're asking for not guilty verdicts, but because they're warranted."

• • •

When Mitch returns home at the noon break, he shakes his head as he relates the substance of Gleason's opening statement.

"He's twisted everything," Mitch says dejectedly.

"You don't think the jury will believe Juan *if* he takes the stand?" I ask.

"The operative word is *when*," Mitch replies. "The defense has no choice but to call him to the stand. Without his testimony there is no defense. It's not unusual to put the police officers on trial when the testimony of a defendant differs from that of the police officers. Happens all the time. Remember the O.J. Simpson case?"

"It's obvious Juan will have to perjure himself," I muse, chewing on a hangnail.

"Not if the police officers indeed planted the evidence as Gleason contends."

I'm stunned thinking Mitch would even harbor or entertain such a thought. "You don't really believe that do you?" I ask.

"Hell, no!" Mitch blurts. "If Gleason was told by his client that happened and the only testimony to refute it is that of the police officers, specifically Connors and Lewis, the ones accused of having planted the evidence, he can certainly rely on what his client has told him. That's a credibility issue for the jury."

Now I'm getting anxious. Could Juan beat the system? "Aren't there a few too many coincidences to explain?" I ask.

"Hopefully, the jury won't be that gullible," Mitch says reflectively.

"If Gleason is that gullible, then why wouldn't a jury follow suit?" I ask.

Taking my hand in his, Mitch says, "Sam, filing charges and proving a criminal case, particularly a capital case, are as different as night and day. If the jury has any reasonable doubt, they will have no choice but to acquit. That's how our system works!"

I examine the intense look on Mitch's handsome face. "Mitch," I say, "there's something that's always bothered me about you, even more so now."

Mitch releases my hand and asks in a more jovial tone, "Okay, what's that? Remember, I can always plead the Fifth."

"I'm serious," I reply. "You, being the son and grandson of attorneys, why didn't you go to law school? You know more about the law than most attorneys I know."

"How many attorneys do you know?"

"I'm related by marriage to two," I reply with a smile.

"Touché!"

"You haven't answered my question," I persist. "Why didn't you go to law school?"

"Short answer. If I had followed in the footsteps of two prominent attorneys, I would be under tremendous pressure to succeed and if I did it would be considered to be because of them and if I failed, despite them."

"I don't know about that. The Mitch I know is capable of standing on his own two feet. Why, you could even have ran for and been elected President." Mitch emits a loud guffaw. "Wow! You're a very intuitive woman. However, piloting the desk in the oval office couldn't possibly compare to piloting my Navy Hornet. The latter is a hell of a lot more exhilarating."

Liking his answer, I say, "And besides, if you

had become rich and famous, we'd never have met."

"Who knows! You'll always be my First Lady regardless of what title I hold or how rich and famous I become!"

"Good answer."

• • •

The series of witnesses presented by the prosecution spilled into the third week. According to Mitch, the direct was overshadowed by the cross-examination by Gleason who succeeded in questioning the motives of Connors and Lewis and the desire of the authorities to solve what they considered alarming crimes and to find a scapegoat. Since there were no eyewitnesses and the cause of death even a debatable issue, things didn't look too good for the prosecution.

In presenting the case for the defense, Gleason did not dilute his case by inconsequential witnesses. It was obvious Juan had been well coached. He did not appear to be evasive or arrogant. In essence, he acted as one would expect a person wrongfully accused to act. Even Mitch was scratching his head when I asked if Juan's testimony was believable.

"Juan's testimony was convincing and maybe even compelling," Mitch laments. "Even the cross-examination of Juan by Turnbow only bolstered the defense's claims." After a pause, Mitch added, "I'm glad I'm not on the jury."

Suddenly, I'm incensed and blurt, "Does that mean you don't think Juan is the serial killer and may not be my attacker?"

"Hell, no!" It only means I can see a jury finding him not guilty because of the questionable evidence of guilt. Neither my gut feeling or that of a jury counts."

The euphoria I felt when Juan was taken into custody evaporated. My voice quivered when I asked, "You mean he could be exonerated and released back into society?"

Mitch's look was all the answer I needed.

• • •

Apparently, Mitch was not the only one who felt the prosecution had failed to meet its burden of proving Juan's guilt beyond a reasonable doubt. After almost two days of deliberations, the jury returned verdicts of not guilty on all four counts. Whether it was a matter of the authorities skewing the evidence in order to solve killings that may not have been killings at all but unfortunate drownings or an effort to quell public hysteria, the jury when interviewed gave no hint.

"We'll have to tighten security," Mitch says referring to my safety. "I had an eerie feeling while Juan testified that he relished in deception and was not through with his quest to eradicate the world of the Jezebels. I hope I'm wrong."

"Are you saying I'm a Jezebel?" I ask and give him *that* look.

"You'll have to admit all the victims are beautiful," Mitch says and counters me with that *gotcha* look.

"Checkmate!" I say. "If not President of the United States, my dear, with your charming ways, you'd make a great Secretary of State. Diplomacy is in your DNA."

Chapter Sixteen

Fallout

Hoping to catch the verdict as soon as it's announced, Mitch and I keep the TV on as we go about our daily chores. Our interest isn't just morbid curiosity—we have a horse in this race because of the two attempts made on my life.

"...after two days of deliberation, the twelve-person jury returned verdicts of not guilty on all four charges..." was all I heard the newscaster say before my legs give out and I collapse. Mitch is immediately at my side.

"Sam, Sam! What is it?" Mitch asks as he helps me onto the sofa.

I point to the TV and stammer, "Not guilty, Mitch. They found him not guilty on all counts," is all I could manage to say.

"What!" Mitch sits down beside me and running his fingers through his hair, he murmurs, "Although we kinda prepared for it, it's still a shock. How could they..."

"Don't know. Now what do we do? I don't feel safe here anymore."

"Damned if I'm going to let that creep run us

off. We're going to stay and fight! That's what we're going to do!" Mitch says, and I suspect that his determined tone of voice is the same he used as he led his squad into combat and emerged victorious.

Before I could respond, our attention was directed back to the TV. The protestors must have been prepared for whatever way the verdict went. It was like watching ants suddenly appear out of nowhere to claim their share of the picnic scraps. With placards in hand and a crowd just as large as any political rally, the demonstrators took over the steps and street in front of the courthouse. We watched Turnbow being protected by a police escort as he exited the building.

The mob gathered in clusters and shouted obscenities. They drowned out the news reporters who attempted to narrate the events. They waved placards with their disparaging messages boldly displayed in large letters. *Racist* was written on some of the placards and shouted by the demonstrators as Turnbow and his entourage made their way through the crowd. Other placards read: *White Supremist* and *Defund the Police*. One even demanded that Connors and Lewis be fired and that Turnbow be impeached.

The police department which was in the same block as the courthouse, was experiencing the same treatment. In fact, the mob grew in size before our eyes as Mitch and I watched in horror. Soon the entire block was swarming with irate protestors banning together to create disruption and hate. Concern was elevated when the noisy demonstration turned violent. Several police cruisers parked on the street in front of the police station were set ablaze and the crowd began throwing missiles which were readily at hand, such as rocks and water bottles.

• • •

"Oh, no!" I exclaimed as we watched Juan exit the courthouse. Just seeing him made my skin crawl.

Mitch put his arm around my shoulders and held me close. "Easy, Sam, I'm here. I'll protect you." Then gritting his teeth, Mitch whispered, his eyes glued to the TV as he watched Juan descend the courthouse steps, "Not on my watch, you bastard, not on my watch!"

• • •

Heralded by the demonstrators as a victim and a hero, Juan reveled in all the glory. The hero worshipers shouted words of praise for him having bucked the system and having emerged triumphant. It was David against Goliath. His sudden elevation to stardom boggled his mind and he postured for the television crews unabashed.

"How do you feel having been acquitted?" a reporter asks sticking a mic into Juan's face.

With Gleason at his side, Juan took the mic in his hand, and began to shout obscenities aimed at the police, the DA, and the criminal justice system in general. His denunciation of the criminal justice system and everyone connected with it was interrupted by chants of encouragement and loud applause by the boisterous demonstrators. The longer he spoke the more emboldened he became. The same was true of the demonstrators. It was obvious Juan relished in all the attention he was receiving. Maybe his weapon of choice was rhetoric. Maybe trading extermination of the Jezebels for fame was not such a bad thing. Little did he know of all the fame and fortune that awaited him.

"Are you going to sue for false arrest?" another reporter asks.

Juan looks at Gleason. "Too soon to even consider," Gleason replies as he speaks into the live mic.

"What are your plans now?" a third reporter quires.

Again, Juan looks at Gleason. "Juan's going to try to piece his life back together. Now if you'll excuse us…" Gleason says and urges Juan in the direction of the parking lot.

The coverage of the acquittal was tantamount to a feeding frenzy. All of the media outlets jumped on the bandwagon to vilify the law enforcement agencies whether involved in the case or not. The only newspaper that advocated that violence was not an accepted method of dissent and opposed governance by a few was the *Key West Communiqué*. With Jack Evans back on staff, its mantra *fair and accurate*, drove its coverage of Juan's trial, verdict and the fallout. An example was the editorial that appeared in the publication the day following that labeled the riot what it was. Curious enough, all the other news outlets referred to the mob action as a *peaceful demonstration*.

A COMMUNITY DIVIDED

Usually a grand jury indictment is indicative of what a trial jury will later do. But not in the case of the recently concluded multiple murder prosecution in the deaths of Carmen Ochoa, Elana Alverez, Marlene Chambers and Maria Concha. As the attorney representing Juan Santiago argued to the jury, "charges do not equate to a conviction."

In Santiago's three-week trial, almost three dozen witnesses were called by the prosecution. There were no eyewitnesses to the actual killings and the prosecution was based mainly on circumstantial evidence. The evidence that was presented by the prosecution was claimed by the defense to have been planted by two of the investigative police officers, Liam Connors and James Lewis.

The only witness called by the defense was the person charged, Juan Santiago. That's thirty-six against one. Yet, despite the grand jury indictment and the disparity in the number of witnesses, Juan Santiago was acquitted. If Juan Santiago was innocent, then the system worked. If he was guilty, then it didn't.

The editorial board for the **Key West Communiqué** *is at a loss as to why the the acquittal sparked the riot that marks its second day again with violence and destruction of property. Even if Juan Santiago had been found guilty, there are procedures in place to rectify an ill-founded verdict. Surely the demonstrators are not contending the verdict was ill-founded. Remember, only the defense can appeal an adverse verdict. And no matter what evidence turns up in the future pointing to Juan Santiago's* *involvement in the deaths of the four victims, he can't be retried. So, what's the beef?*

If Juan Santiago had the presumption of innocence, so why not the investigating police officers who are claimed to have planted the evidence? Do they possess any less protected rights than anyone else? Isn't it a lot more difficult to prove someone didn't do something than to prove that they did? How do you prove a negative? What proof is there the evidence was planted?

Our newspaper has covered a number of trials where Liam Connors and James Lewis were key prosecution witnesses. In none of them was it ever claimed they did anything improper. Their credibility was never challenged nor are we presumptuous enough now to question it. Our advice to the rioters: Let the justice system run its course. Treat our police the way you'd want to be treated. Next time you call 911, make sure there is someone who can take the call. Better yet, if you think you can do a better job, apply for a position at the PD because there will be plenty of openings should you get your wish with respect to officers Connors and Lewis.

Politicians, being what they are, that is scapegoats subject to public outcry when things don't go well, were being subjected to unreasonable demands, and as expected, it wasn't long before Connors and Lewis were placed on the hot seat. Both detectives were summoned to explain their actions before the Chief of Police and a panel of the Chief's choosing. When Connors and Lewis appear before the disciplinary board of the police department, they are armed with a copy of all the investigative reports relating to the murders of Carmen Ochoa, Elana Alverez, Marlene Chambers and Maria Concha. The board consists of the Chief of Police, Debra Polley, and four senior detectives of the Key West Police Department.

Connors and Lewis sit side-by-side in the hearing room waiting for the procedure to commence. They're still reeling from the adverse ruling in Juan's criminal prosecution and are second-guessing their chosen career paths.

"Should've listened to my dad. He wanted me to become a doctor like him," Connors laments.

"I hear ya," Lewis replies. "My father wanted me to become a priest. Probably wouldn't have worked anyway. Don't think I could forgive killers…"

Both Connors and Lewis grew up with the

current chief, Debra Polley, and they all attended the police academy together. When the prior chief of police retired, all three were on the short list to replace him. The feminine movement was just getting legs and the mayor stated it was time to appoint a female as chief. Debra Polley, being extremely competent and someone who started at the bottom and worked her way up, was the ideal choice regardless of her gender. She was readily accepted by the force including Connors and Lewis. Although she was selected over them, they felt she deserved to be respected. Female or male, it didn't make any difference. She was well qualified for the position.

The room became hushed when Chief Polley entered. "Detectives Connors and Lewis, are you ready to proceed?" she asks in an authoritative tone as she takes a seat at the head of the conference table.

"We are," the two reply in unison.

"To save time, the board proposes to combine your two cases. Do either of you have any objection?"

Again, in unison, both reply "no."

Polley nods and takes a sip of water. It's obvious she's uncomfortable with presiding over this disciplinary action. Toying with the pen she is holding, she begins, "It has come to the board's attention that the two of you may have engaged in unprofessional conduct by planting evidence to obtain a conviction. The case I have reference to is *People v. Juan Santiago* as you've already been advised. Do the two of you realize why you're here and that sanctions for misconduct include suspension or outright dismissal?"

Again, in unison, both reply "yes."

"Very well," Polley says with a grave expression, "Before we begin, do you admit or deny the allegation?"

"Deny," each says.

Adjusting the folders on the table before her, Chief Polley says, "Detective Connors, why don't you go first. We have a copy of the court transcript of the trial which includes the testimony of the two of you. Since I'm familiar with you both having worked with the two of you for almost ten years and am familiar with your history both here and at the police academy, as well as having been involved in a number of investigations with each of you." Turning a page, the Chief glances at it before continuing, "I'm familiar with your exemplary records and adherence to our departmental ethical standards. Therefore, you need only address issues raised in connection with the Santiago investigation."

When Connors starts to stand, Chief Polley

motions for him to remain seated. Connors nods and rearranges his notes on the table. "If you're more comfortable standing, Detective Connors, feel free to do so. But there is no need to." Chief Polley seems to have softened and even manages a smile albeit a stingy one.

"To begin with," Connors states emphatically, "I never have nor ever will plant evidence to obtain a conviction. Not even where the suspect is thought to be a serial killer.

"In following a lead that the person seen with Maria Concha just prior to her death matched the description we had from other witnesses, we engaged in a follow up investigation. We had previously been told by a different witness that at the times she saw the suspect he was usually wearing a T-shirt advertising a fish distributorship with what she thought was the name Donovan's stenciled on it. When we researched fish distributorships in the area, we found a Dougan's but no Donovan's. Thinking that may be the one, we went to the business establishment and interviewed the owner.

"As you recall, we already had Maria Concha's day planner with the initials J S marking a dinner at the *Nautilus* at six p.m. the date she disappeared. The owner of Dougan's provided us with Juan Santiago's name and address. He also confirmed

Juan Santiago had a pair of tennis shoes which had red paint on them similar to those described by several credible witnesses.

"When we went to arrest Juan Santiago for leaving the scene of an accident and question him about knowing the four victims, he gave us permission to search his premises. That's when we found the distinctive typewriter mentioned in our reports. The other items connected to the four murders were discovered at the same time pursuant to a search warrant issued by a judge. They were buried in the sand in a clump of brush close to Juan Santiago's apartment complex."

Connors pauses long enough to take a sip of water. *It's now or never.* Taking a deep breath, he proceeds. "If we had taken those items from the bodies of the victims, why wouldn't there be a record of that with the custodian of records here at the police station in accordance with departmental policy? To suggest items taken from four different victims on four different occasions and hiding them so that we could plant them on a suspect at a later date is absurd. Those items would have helped our department solve those crimes if we had them analyzed at the time the victims' bodies were autopsied. If we had the distinctive typewriter in our custody prior to finding it in Juan Santiago's apartment, that would mean Detective Lewis and I had typed and sent the notes to the *Key West Communiqué* after each of the murders. If we planted the items that only the killer possessed, which we didn't, then maybe we should be charged with the crimes."

Sensing Connors was becoming agitated, Lewis cleared his throat loudly in an attempt to signal Connors to back off. Connors got the message and leaned back in his chair indicating he had concluded his defense.

Apparently, Chief Polley also picked up on Lewis' cautionary action. Before moving on, she says, "Is there anything further you'd like to add, Detective Connors?"

Glancing at Lewis, Connors says, "I would be willing to submit to a polygraph before I resign."

"I don't think that will be necessary," Chief Polley says in a more conciliatory tone. "But first let me ask Detective Lewis if his explanation would be substantially the same as yours."

Before even being asked the question, Lewis answers, "It would be the same. The absurdity of Juan Santiago's defense is evident from the circumstances. If this board subscribes to that absurdity as did the jury, then you have my resignation as well."

Chief Polley looks sternly at the two detectives seated before her. "Before the two of you do anything rash, would you mind waiting in the hall while I confer with the other members of the panel?" she asks.

"Not at all," Connors replies. Lewis nods his agreement.

Once alone in the hallway, Lewis grins at Connors, "Proud of you, buddy—even if it means I may have to consider a career change."

"Yeah, me, too…" Connors mumbles. "But I love being a detective."

"Don't we both!" Lewis says, and the sadness in his voice is unmistakable.

Their banter was cut short when moments later the two were summoned back into the hearing room.

"After hearing your statements and considering the circumstances surrounding your investigations and treatment of Juan Santiago, we find no wrong doing on your part and not only do we not condemn you but we commend you on your upholding your oaths to defend and protect and uphold the constitution and laws of our state and federal governments. The board is proud of each of you! With that having been said, we hereby stand adjourned."

Connors and Lewis sit in stunned silence as

the members of the panel approach and shake their hands. "Keep up the good work and stay safe out there," Chief Polley says as she passes behind them on her way out the door.

. . .

Juan, being the hero and the center of attention, is in seventh heaven. Not only has he slain the giant, but he has garnered the admiration of his peers. His support comes from all over the country and from groups he never heard of. The same is true of the funds that keep pouring in. Juan deposits the contributions into his bank account and is surprised at the rate his bottom line is increasing. He no longer is a nobody or destitute. He exacted his perceived pound of flesh and has nothing further to prove— not to himself; not to anyone else. He's suddenly in great demand at various anti-government rallies and is hoarding cash, classic automobiles, and women as if they were canned goods.

One of his new contacts flies him to Cuba to visit his family. Juan also receives a hero's welcome in Cuba which adds to his feeling of invincibility. He hits the night spots with his newfound friends and the sky's the limit. While dancing with and putting the moves on a Carmen lookalike at a local casino, he is challenged by the Carmen lookalike's suiter. In his euphoric state of mind,

Juan must have forgotten about how jealous Cuban men or any men for that matter can be about their women. What transpired in the alley behind the cantina was not pretty. Juan, in his half drunken state, was outmatched. Fired by jealous rage, the stranger rearranged Juan's face with a razor-sharp knife. After the fight, Juan was left for dead in the alley. However, when his hanger-on drinking companions found him, and he was still breathing, they rushed him to a hospital. After all, he was their golden goose.

Juan was close to death from loss of blood when he was admitted to the emergency room. A team of skilled doctors managed to save him and several days later, he was removed from the critical care list and referred to a plastic surgeon. Dr. Rico Herrera, Juan was told, was the best in Havana, or all of Cuba for that matter.

• • •

"There has been much damage to the muscles and nerves in your face," Dr. Herrera advises Juan. "Although I can make you whole again, I cannot restore you to your former self." After a long pause, Dr. Herrera asks, "Are you willing to live with a totally new face?"

"Si," Juan replies. "In fact, I'd welcome a complete change. How long do you think it will take before I'm healed?"

"Many, many months. The reconstruction is a slow process, and we cannot rush it."

"Okay by me. Let's get started right away," Juan says.

"Ah, about the fee?" Dr. Herrera asks.

"Huh! Oh, the fee. No problem, Doc. I have plenty. You do a good job and I'll see that you get a nice bonus."

· · ·

The months that followed found Juan in and out of multiple surgeries and excruciating pain. During his lucid hours, he plotted a return visit to Key West to take care of old business. Because of all that has happened to him, he is now completely demented and blames *Cuatro* for his misfortune. He vows to finally even the score with that Jezebel. Risking a lot for a little no longer is a consideration.

· · ·

During the days and months after the trial, Mitch and I were overly cautious knowing Juan Santiago was free. Finally, one day as we sit on the patio, Mitch blurts, "Sam, I can't take it much longer. I'm tired of looking over my shoulder and jumping at every strange sound. I'm going to call Connors to see if he knows where the creep is."

"Then what?" I ask.

"I'll confront the creep, that's what! Even though the authorities are prohibited from beating a confession out of the bastard, I not only can but will."

"Don't forget who you're dealing with. Remember, he's a loony-tune, unpredictable and has the mindset of a suicide bomber. Please, just let the police do their job!"

Mitch slumps back in his chair. "You're right—as always." He then adds, "What if we move?"

"Where can we go that he couldn't find us?" I ask. "I understand he has mucho dinero in donations from various cop-hater and antigovernment organizations who think he's their messiah."

Attila stretches out at Mitch's feet and Mitch leans over and scratches the dog's head. Attila whines as Mitch stands. "I'm going to call Connors anyway," Mitch says. "Down deep, I guess I have no choice but to have faith in the system!"

• • •

"Hey, Mitch!" Connors answers. "To what do I owe the pleasure?"

"If you describe receiving a call from a nervous wreck *a pleasure*." Mitch says sarcastically and cuts to the chase. "Sam and I are constantly on pins and needles and we jump at every unusual sound. You have any idea where Santiago has disappeared to?"

"Nothing concrete. I checked with Gleason a couple of months ago and he told me the last he heard Juan had gone back to Cuba."

"Yeah, that's only ninety miles away so that's of little consolation," Mitch replies.

"Sorry I can't do any better than that, Mitch," says Connors.

"Not your fault," Mitch replies. "See patrol cars out this way occasionally and know you're doing everything you can."

• • •

After Mitch hangs up, I ask, "What's the latest?"

"Connors says, that according to Gleason, Juan's thought to be back in Cuba."

"Even if he were in Siberia, that wouldn't be far enough away." I say and then add, "I've been thinking, Mitch."

"That's dangerous," Mitch teases. "What've you been thinking?"

"About the baby we keep putting off—"

"Oh, no! Not that again," Mitch groans.

"Yes, that again!" I snap. "Come on, Mitch. Are we going to give that pervert the satisfaction of controlling our lives?" When Mitch looks down at his hands, I bark, "And don't you look away when I'm talking to you!"

"It's not you, honey," he says and looks up. "It's

a situation I can't control, and I don't like it either. You know I love you with my whole being. Your safety is my first concern!"

"And I love you, too. That's why we have to live our lives forward and not backward. I'm rapidly closing in on thirty. I want to start a family before I get too old to have children."

Mitch takes my hand in his. "Sure, if it means that much to you, I'm all for it." We both become emotional.

• • •

Approximately nine months later, Alexander Mitchel McElroy arrives. After the birth, Mitch sits by my hospital bed cradling little Alex in his arms. The smile on Mitch's face lights up the room.

"Thanks, honey. You were right. We needed this little guy to complete our lives."

"We're not done yet!" I say and watch for Mitch's expression to change.

Surprisingly, he says, "How 'bout an even dozen?"

"Not until science finds a way for men to have babies," I say and flash a broad smile. When Mitch just groans, I say, "Why not? You keep telling me what an easy life women have. Now's your opportunity to change places!"

Chapter Seventeen

Déjà Vu

After months of surgery, the bandages are removed from Juan's face and he is finally allowed to examine himself in a mirror.

"Whoa! Is this really me!" he exclaims, barely able to contain his excitement. He then makes faces apparently in an effort to verify that the image in the mirror is actually the reconstructed Juan Santiago.

"Yes, it's really you," Dr. Herrera replies with a broad smile. "How'd I do?"

Pointing to the nightstand beside the bed, Juan says, "Hand me my checkbook and I'll show you." Juan then writes a personal check to Dr. Herrera in the amount of twenty thousand dollars.

Dr. Herrera raises his brow as he accepts the check. "That's quite a tip," he remarks.

"And you're worth every penny," Juan replies. "How soon can I get outta here?"

"First thing tomorrow, if you want. I'll take care of the release paperwork this afternoon."

• • •

The following day, after being released from the hospital, Juan takes the first flight from Cuba to Miami. He arrives in Miami early enough to catch the ferry returning to Key West. He grabs the same seat he had before and smiles as he relives his encounter with Elana Alverez, victim number three, on this same ferry. Except for looks, he's back to his old mindset.

Upon arrival in Key West, he stands on the pier surveilling familiar surroundings. After almost two years, he's surprised that not much has changed. He's eager to encounter old acquaintances to test his new face. If Jackson, the bartender at the *Half Shell* doesn't recognize him, nobody will.

• • •

"Afternoon, Sir," Jackson greets Juan when he enters the cool, dimly lit bar.

"Afternoon," Juan replies and looks the bartender straight in the eyes. "I'll have a Corona and half dozen raw oysters," Juan says, and waits for any sign of recognition. There is none.

"Coming right up," Jackson says as he wipes his hands on the bar towel. "You from these parts?" he asks as he processes the order. Juan shakes his head hoping to dissuade further conversation. Jackson takes the hint.

After polishing off the beer and oysters, Juan heads out into the late afternoon sun. He has a spring in his step knowing he is completely transformed and can go anywhere he wants without being recognized. I've some unfinished business to tend to, he says to himself and whistles an unrecognizable tune as he swaggers off down the street.

• • •

Alex is now fifteen months old. He has been walking for the last five months and at times is hard to keep up with. Mitch, in his excited exuberance, erected a play set for his son even before Alex started walking. If Mitch is disappointed, it doesn't show when it appears Attila seems to have shifted his affection from Mitch to Alex. Attila is the baby's constant companion when we're outside and very protective of him.

It's late afternoon, and as I wait for Mitch to return from the airfield after taking the Piper for a spin, I'm entertaining Alex by gently pushing him in his childproof swing.

"More, Mommy, more," Alex pleads when I attempt to take him inside.

"Okay, five more minutes then it's time for your bath." I know he doesn't understand but he gives me that Mitch-like smile that crumbles my resolve. I have been leaving my cellphone on the patio table when playing with Alex after having lost it once in the sandbox. When it rings, I think it's Mitch and I rush to answer it leaving Alex still in his swing.

When I reach for the phone, I hear footsteps and a shadow crosses the patio table. I look up and don't recognize the man standing there but something about him seems familiar.

"Hello, *Cuatro*," the man says. My blood runs cold when I recognize his voice. "It's been awhile…"

I'm paralyzed with fear. However, my first thought is for Alex and I glance in the direction of the swing. He's safe, at least for the time being.

Apparently, following my gaze, Psycho-man says, "Don't worry about your brat. My beef is with you, you Jezebel. You ruined my life and I'm here to prove payback is hell!"

When I look toward the swing, I notice Attila, bearing his teeth and emitting a low growl. He's standing close to Alex. My instincts kick in as I remember the command and I shout, "STRIKE!" With lightning speed, Attila races toward the patio and grabs Juan by the leg. Juan yells and falls backward hitting his head hard on the cement tiles. As soon as Juan hits the tiles, Attila grabs him by the neck and sinks his teeth deep. Blood gushes from Juan's neck as Attila continues to maul him. Horrified, I watch Juan keep up the struggle for a few moments and then go limp. Judging from the amount of blood, I conclude Attila must have hit the jugular vein.

"Mommy," I hear Alex cry and when I look around, I see Mitch rushing in my direction. He's holding Alex and covers the distance between us in two strides and gathers me in his free arm.

"Are you alright?" he asks.

"Yes, I think so. Everything happened so fast, I…" Then looking down at Juan's lifeless body, I ask, "Is he dead?"

"I certainly hope so," Mitch replies and hands me the baby. He then kneels and checks Juan for a pulse. After a moment he looks up and shakes his head.

"I thought you were flying the Piper," I say.

"Had a premonition," Mitch says as tears form.

"Thank God for premonitions," I say as Mitch places the 911 call.

• • •

The next day Connors pays us another visit. "The deceased's fingerprints return to one Juan Santiago," he announces. "Autopsy revealed he had some extensive plastic surgery during the two years he spent in Cuba." Connors then bends and pets Attila who has been vying for attention and adds, "Attila must have recognized his scent immediately, which just proves, even though you can change your looks, you can't change your scent.

A skunk, by any other name, is still a skunk."

Connors bids us ado then bounds down the steps to where Lewis is waiting for him in the cruiser. Connors waves to us as they pull away. Lewis honks.

"Think we'll ever see them again," I ask as we both wave back.

"I hope not," Mitch replies. "I certainly hope not, unless it's under different circumstances." Then after a brief pause, he adds, "With both Connors and Lewis having added to their families about the same time Alex was born, our paths will no doubt pass either on a baseball diamond, a basketball court or a football field in the not too distant future."

"How about the tennis court?" I ask. "As I recall, both their new additions are girls."

"Then our paths will cross when the kids play mixed doubles," Mitch responds.

• • •

It is not long before the three couples, along with their offspring become fast friends and spend a lot of time together. The bad memories fade as new memories are made. *If God be with us, who can be against us!*

Finishing Touches

Having solved the lookalike murders, Connors goes over his final report. Satisfied it's complete, he puts the file in his Out-basket to be placed in the box marked Juan Santiago. He then stands, puts on his jacket, and heads for Lewis' office.

"Hey, you busy?" he asks as he raps on the open door with his knuckles.

"Never too busy for you," Lewis chirps. "What's up?"

"We have some calls to make. Come on, I'm driving." Connors watches Lewis cringe. "Okay then, you drive," Connors says and hands Lewis the keys.

Once they're buckled in the police cruiser, Lewis asks, "Where to?"

"Need to take a run past *Bling*," Connors answers.

"Did we miss something?"

"Nope. Just keeping my promise to Mary Alice," Connors says and smiles at his partner.

"Okay if I wait in the car?" Lewis teases. "I don't like being seen in *boutiques*. You know how rumors start."

• • •

When Connors enters the shop, Kitty is standing behind the counter organizing some jewelry items. She is barely recognizable. Her hair is now back to natural blond, her pink braces have been removed and her jeans no longer have tears in the knees. She spots him immediately.

"Afternoon, detective. If you're here on official business, I want you to know I gave up weed and have enrolled in college. My parents keep telling me I'm not the same person!"

"Good for you, Kitty. You'll be glad you did. And I'm not here on official business." Connors then begins looking around at the displays.

"Can I help you find something?" Kitty offers.

"I'm looking for a bracelet. You have something appropriate for a six or seven-year-old?"

"Indeed we do!" Kitty chirps as she rounds the counter and motions for Connors to follow her. She leads him to a rack of colorful bracelets and stands aside. "These are our bestsellers," she says.

With so many to chose from, Connors just stares at the items. Apparently noticing the bewildered expression on his face, Kitty asks, "What does the child like?"

"Well, she has a dog…"

"Perfect!" Kitty remarks and slowly turns the rack closely examining the bracelets as they pass by. "Ha! Here it is," she says as she removes a pink and white beaded bracelet strung on an elastic band. The focal point is a small silver poodle charm.

"I'll take it!" Connors says emphatically and adds, "Can I get it gift wrapped?"

• • •

Carefully carrying the elaborately wrapped small box containing the bracelet, Connors joins Lewis who has been waiting in the cruiser. Lewis glances at the gift box and smiles. "She's just going to flip," Lewis says. "Even if the box were empty, the wrapping would be a party all by itself."

"Yeah, Kitty has a knack alright," Connors replies, then after a pause, he adds, "Tying up loose ends is the part of the job I really like."

"Okay then, let's go play Santa Claus!" says Lewis.

• • •

As the detectives exit the building leaving a delighted Mary Alice admiring her gift, Connors says to Lewis, "I'll pop for lunch."

"Works for me. Where to?" Lewis asks as he buckles his seatbelt.

"The *Nautilus*," Connors answers.

Lewis looks surprised. "That's pretty fancy for

a quick lunch…"

"I know but we need to explain to Jimmy that because Santiago wasn't convicted, he can't collect a Crime Stopper reward."

"A phone call would work—"

"Not my style," Connors interrupts. "I like to show my appreciation in person." Conveying disappointing news is the part of tying up loose ends I don't particularly relish."

Looking disappointed, Jimmy says he understands and thanks the officers for coming by in person to tell him.

When they finish lunch, Lewis goes to the parking lot to retrieve the car as Connors waits in line to pay the check. When the cashier hands him the credit card receipt to sign, he adds a $50 tip for Jimmy.

• • •

"Well, since we're on a mission to tie up loose ends, mind if we stop by Sammy's and bring him up to date?" Lewis asks.

Imitating Sammy, Connors says, "Shore, why not?"

When they arrive at the vacant lot, Sammy's tent is no longer there. Perplexed, Lewis says, "Wonder if he relocated? I bet Bethany knows what happened to him."

The detectives find Bethany in her rose garden. No surprise there. Lewis approaches her.

"Afternoon, Ms. Oglesby," he says.

"Why, Officer Lewis. You startled me."

"Sorry, ma'am, didn't mean to startle you. Went by Sammy's and he's apparently moved. Any idea where he's gone?"

"Yes. Just last Wednesday he stopped by my place. He told me some official people came to talk to him. He said they determined he was eligible for VA benefits since he was a Korean war veteran, and that they would be moving him into an apartment."

"Do you know where?" Lewis asks.

"Sammy said he was moving to that new apartment complex over on Lexington."

"Thanks, Ms. Oglesby," Lewis replies and turns to leave.

"Oh, by the way, officer…,"

Lewis turns back, "Yes?"

"Sammy's name really is Samuel Culpepper. He told me he retired with a rank of sergeant but liked the way Colonel sounded better."

"Well, I'll be damned!" Lewis blurts. "Oh, sorry ma'am. We'll be sure to use his preferred title when we speak to him. He deserves the respect."

"That was my reaction as well," Bethany says and before returning to her gardening says, "They're in the midst of constructing a new McDonald's across from Sammy's apartment complex."

• • •

Lewis joins Connors who has been waiting in the cruiser. "Everything alright?" Connors asks, apparently noticing tears forming in Lewis' eyes.

"Yep! Everything's just fine," Lewis says. "Everything's just fine and dandy!" He then puts the car in gear, "Let's stop by Sammy's new digs and then go catch some bad guys."